mɪssɪng
ellen

'A tense and tender portrayal of
friendship and loss. *Missing Ellen* is
beautifully written and
completely addictive.'
Laura Jane Cassidy, author of Angel Kiss
and Eighteen Kisses

'*Missing Ellen* is a beautifully-crafted
novel about love, friendship and
everything in between.'
Michelle Gyo, Random House, Germany

'I really enjoyed *Missing Ellen*!
The believable friendship and the
compelling mystery at its core are
really involving. A lovely, simply-
written book about a complex subject.'
Deirdre Sullivan, author of Prim
Improper and Improper Order

D0988095

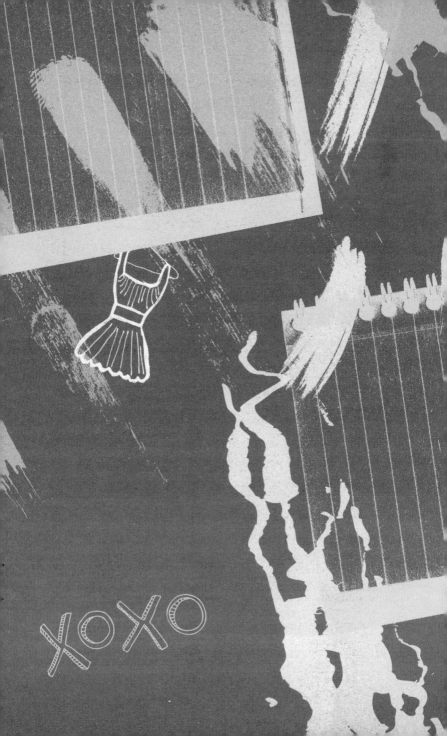

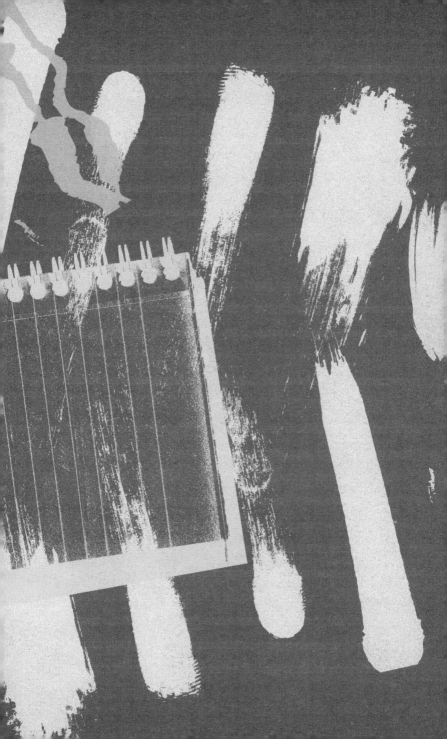

missing
ellen

missing
ellen

*she was already gone
before she walked away ...*

Natasha Mac a' Bháird

THE O'BRIEN PRESS
DUBLIN

First published 2013 by The O'Brien Press Ltd,
12 Terenure Road East, Rathgar, Dublin 6, Ireland.
Tel: +353 1 4923333; Fax: +353 1 4922777
E-mail: books@obrien.ie
Website: www.obrien.ie
ISBN: 978-1-84717-353-9
Copyright for text © Natasha Mac a'Bháird 2013
Copyright for typesetting, layout, design
The O'Brien Press Ltd.

All rights reserved. No part of this publication may be reproduced or utilised in any
form or by any means, electronic or mechanical, including photocopying, recording or
in any information storage and retrieval system, without permission in writing from the
publisher.

1 2 3 4 5 6 7 8 9 10
13 14 15 16 17

Layout and design: The O'Brien Press Ltd.
Printed and bound by CPI Group (UK) Ltd, Croydon, CR0 4YY
The paper in this book is produced using pulp from
managed forests.

Laois County Library
Leabharlann Chontae Laoise

Acc. No. ...... 13|8033 ....

Class No. .... JF ....

Inv. No. ...... 12697 ....

The O'Brien Press receives assistance from

dedication

For my lovely mother, Anne.

Dear Ellen,

I missed you in school today. It's so strange to be starting a new school year without you. Fuddy Duddy was being a complete cow as usual – the summer holidays don't seem to have done her much good. She gave out to me for having too many earrings in. Like she would know anything about fashion. You should have seen the hideous brown blouse she had on today. It was the kind of thing my granny would have given to Oxfam twenty years ago. The colour of Bovril or something horrible like that, with a big frilly collar.

It feels weird to be writing you a letter, but I don't think you will be checking your emails, and I know Mum will be checking mine. So I've found this spiral notebook in the bottom drawer of my desk. The first few pages are filled with sketches of different costumes and outfits, so if Mum picks it up she will take no notice, I hope, and won't flick on through to here. I'll be able to write exactly what I want.

It was David's idea, really. He suggested I should write about what happened, put it all down on paper, a kind of exorcism or something. You're wondering who David is, I know. I'll get back to that. But first I need to go back to the beginning.

Love,

Maggie.

Actually though, I am not really sure when the beginning is, how far back I need to go to make some sort of sense of it all. If that's even possible. Did it all start with what happened to Ellen's family last spring, or did it go even further back?

I can still remember the day I first met Ellen, a bouncy five-year-old, red plaits flying as she dashed from one side of the junior infants classroom to the other, wanting to try everything at once – the books, the sand table, the dolls' corner. I remember being fascinated by her and how utterly fearless she seemed. I was clinging on to my mum's hand, not wanting her to go, not wanting to be left alone in this strange place. And here was this girl, no bigger than me, who seemed completely happy to be there and eager to explore our new world. I thought she was amazing. And strangely enough, she seemed to like me too. She took me under her wing, bossed the other children around and shouted at a little boy who tried to take my snack. And from that moment on we were friends.

I think even then I knew that wherever Ellen is is always the best, the most exciting place to be. She lights up the room with her energy and passion for life. When she leaves, I feel deflated, like everything that was going to happen has happened and there's no point in being there any longer.

But that's too far back, I think. I suppose the best place to start is a dreary Tuesday last spring, Ellen and I in geography with Fuddy Duddy (Mrs Duddy to her face. The nickname was kind of inevitable if she insisted on having that surname combined with a complete lack of any sense of fashion). Ellen trying to pass the time by scribbling notes to me on her homework notebook. And Ellen's father, at home, packing his bags and getting ready to move out for good.

Her mother didn't show up to collect her after school. This wasn't exactly unusual. Mrs Barrett has never been the most reliable of mothers.

'Do you want to give her a ring?' Mum asked Ellen, sounding a little anxious. Mum always leaves in plenty of time to collect us. She was late once a few months back because there were road works along the way. I was almost in tears by the time she arrived, and she wasn't much better. I felt silly afterwards, for panicking like that, but it was just so unlike her.

Ellen shrugged. 'There's no point. She couldn't find her mobile charger this morning, and she never answers the landline in case it's Granny calling for Dad.'

Mum looked kind of shocked at this. I thought she should have been used to Mrs B by now, but I guess she always wants to think the best of people.

'Come on then, I'll give you a lift home,' Mum said.

When we got to the Barretts' house all the curtains at the front windows were closed, but again, it wasn't something all that unusual. Even before Ellen's dad left, her mum was kind of inconsistent. Some days she would be up at the crack of dawn, heading to the gym before coming home to make pancakes from scratch for Ellen and Robert's breakfast. Other days she wouldn't even get up to wave them off to school. It never seemed to bother Ellen. I guess she was used to it.

I think Mum must have sensed that something was wrong though, because she didn't just wait in the car to make sure Ellen had got in OK like she usually does. She got out of the car and went to the door with Ellen, round to the back of the house. I followed them, not sure what else to do.

Robert's bike was lying on its side outside the back door. My dad would have gone crazy, he is forever nagging Jamie and me to put our bikes away so they won't get rusty from the rain. Mum just walked past it and asked Ellen if she had her key. Ellen produced it from where it hung from a chain around her neck – she likes to call herself a latch-key kid – and opened the door. I got this increasing sense of doom, I suppose you could call it. I don't mean to sound melodramatic but I think Mum's nervousness was infecting me or something. Ellen didn't seem to notice anything wrong. She was just humming to herself and twisting her ponytail around her fingers.

Mrs B was sitting at the kitchen table, still in her nightie, her elbows resting among the breakfast dishes. Her hair was all over the place and she was just staring into space. She didn't even seem to hear us come in.

I looked at Mum, not sure how to react. Ellen was already at the table, pulling out a chair and sitting down. 'Mum, what's wrong?' she demanded, shoving aside a bowl of soggy coco pops to take her mum's hand.

Mrs B finally noticed us. She looked at Ellen and gave this chilling, bitter sort of laugh. 'Well he's finally done it, hasn't he? He's left us.'

'What are you talking about?' Ellen sounded angry, but also a little frightened. 'He can't have. He's just being dramatic. He'll be back later.'

'No he won't. Not this time,' Mrs B said quietly. 'He's taken everything with him. Go and see if you don't believe me.'

There was a crash as Ellen knocked over her chair in her haste to run out of the room. Mum put her arm around Mrs B and patted her awkwardly, saying 'There, there', rather as if she were a small child who had bumped her head and not a middle-aged woman whose husband had just left her after twenty years of marriage and two children.

I stood for a moment not quite knowing what to do with my hands, then I went to put on the kettle. That's what Mum normally does when there's some sort of a crisis. Is it just so she will have something to do with her hands? I never thought about that before. I opened the cupboard to take out some mugs, but there weren't any. As quietly as I could I opened the dishwasher – it was full of dirty dishes. I took out four mugs and rinsed them under the tap. Just as I was searching for tea bags Ellen came crashing back into the room.

'He's really being a drama queen this time. His wardrobe is empty, all his CDs, everything.' She started to cry, and I think that must have set Mrs B off, because she started to cry too, and suddenly the two of them were clinging to each other and sobbing. Mum took over the tea-making duties, locating tea bags and milk and even a few broken biscuits from the bottom of the biscuit barrel.

I watched her, feeling selfishly glad that I had a mum who was good at things like making tea in crises, and a nice predictable dad whose idea of doing something really wild was the time he tried to hide his grey hairs with Just for Men. I didn't know what to say to Ellen. I was used to her parents' rows, but this was something new.

There, that's a beginning of sorts, isn't it? David can't say I didn't try.

Dear Ellen,

Fuddy Duddy wore the blouse again today. This time with a frilly skirt in lime green. What on earth was she thinking? She could find nothing wrong with my appearance today (I took out the extra earrings and hid them in my pencil case before I went in) so she decided to complain about my homework instead. Apparently my essay on rock formation was 'long, rambling and lacking in purpose'. You would think she would be pleased. It sounds exactly like a description of one of her classes.

Siobhan Brady has started a list at the back of her homework notebook of boys she wants to snog this year. What is she like? Should we warn them, do you think? Roll up, roll up, all you young men. Don't just become a notch on someone's bedpost. Become a tick on Siobhan Brady's list instead!

PE today was hideous. Pouring rain all day, and Miss O'Neill decides it's a good idea to play camogie. 'We don't call it an all-weather pitch for nothing, girls,' she trills in this silly fake voice. So we all trudge out onto the pitch in our stupid white shorts and T-shirts and run around for forty minutes, no real idea where the ball is at any time – it's raining so hard we can barely see each other never mind the ball – and jump every time she blows that stupid whistle. Of course the sporty girls thought it was great fun and spent the whole class trying to outdo each other and see who could impress Miss O'Neill the most. While the rest of us mere mortals tried to hover in the background, saving our bouts of energy for quickly dodging in the opposite direction any time it seemed like the ball might be coming our way. I found myself wishing I was sitting at my desk at the back of maths class watching Bouncer draw isosceles triangles on the board. Yes, it was that bad.

Last week, of course, there was blazing sunshine, and instead of taking us outside to work on our tans while pretending to play camogie, Miss O'Neill thought it would be a good idea to run laps around the stuffy gym. She must have been some sort of dictator in a former life. Or maybe a nun.

Siobhan put Liam's name on her list. Silly cow. Like he has eyes for anyone but you.

Love,

Maggie.

Ellen's parents have been arguing for as long as I can remember. When we were seven, things were particularly bad. Her house was always filled with tension. You could almost feel it when you walked in the front door. You know how some houses have a warm comforting smell, like vegetable stew simmering on the hob, and some are filled with noise, with lots of children running about, a radio blasting in the background, a mum shouting to the kids to keep it down. In Ellen's house nothing struck me as much as that atmosphere of people disliking each other.

Ellen would keep coming over to my house to escape. She never seemed upset by the way her parents behaved, she just acted crazier than ever. One day she persuaded me that we should turn all my dolls into clowns by painting their faces and have our own three-ring circus (my room, the landing and Jamie's room being the three rings). We got out my paints and set to work decorating our little clowns – orange for the background, purples and reds and blues around the eyes and mouths. We took off all their pretty dresses, put them in plain white vests belonging to me and then painted those too. They looked absolutely awful by the time we'd finished with them, but we thought they were brilliant – the perfect clowns. Jamie woke up from his nap as we took over his room, but instead of crying he just sat up and watched us. Ellen was delighted to have an audience and started making her clowns turn somersaults and squirt each other with water, making Jamie laugh with delight.

Afterwards, I felt so sorry for my dolls, with their sad little painted faces which were never really the same, even after I'd scrubbed and scrubbed them. They're in a box in the attic now. Poor little things – most of them still have a distinctly orange hue.

My mum didn't even get cross with us, I think she knew what was going on in Ellen's house. She asked her if she wanted to stay for dinner and even rang up her mum to see if she could stay the night. It was our first proper sleepover and we marked the occasion by having a midnight feast (chocolate biscuits, crisps and buns smuggled upstairs and hidden in my doll's pram). We were just getting into the *Malory Towers* books and thought we were just like the girls in those, though it was a pity we didn't have a swimming pool to have our feast beside, or a mad French teacher to hide from.

We waited and waited for midnight to come around – it wouldn't have been a proper midnight feast if we'd had it any earlier – and I kept falling asleep, but each time Ellen woke me up by throwing a teddy at me, until all her teddies were gone. Finally we heard the clock in the hall striking midnight and we scrambled out of bed to raid the pram. We'd forgotten to bring anything to drink so I sneaked out to the bathroom and filled two toothbrush glasses with water. That was when Ellen thought of doing the vow. She got me to loop my arm around hers like people do with champagne glasses. I spilled some of the water on my pyjamas but I didn't say anything, I didn't want her thinking I was a spoilsport.

'Repeat after me,' Ellen said solemnly. 'I swear that I, Maggie, will be best friends with Ellen now and until the end of time, and that nothing shall come between us.' I think she'd mixed up the Barbie wedding film with a bedtime prayer. I repeated it just as seriously and we drank the slightly minty-tasting water from our toothbrush glasses.

Dear Ellen,

My mum doesn't know what to make of me these days. She keeps fussing over me, offering lifts, checking over and over to see what time I'll be home, and I just lose patience with her.

She's always been a total worrier of course, but since it happened her crazy overprotective mother thing has gone into overdrive. It's almost as if she feels vindicated for having been so paranoid all these years.

I get so fed up listening to her. It's not like I'm even going anywhere anyway – just school, for God's sake. What's the point in going anywhere else without you? So eventually I'll snap at her, and then she'll look at me like she really doesn't know me at all. Because the truth is, I've never been any trouble. I'm so good it's embarrassing. I've never been grounded or anything like that, and even in those last few months, when you were dragging me into one drama after another, I somehow managed not to get caught. And Mum and I have always got along. She always used to say I'm the kind of daughter any mother would be proud to have.

And now? Well, it's not exactly normal, is it? I mean, I doubt she tells the ladies at her coffee mornings about me seeing David, or any of that. Now she's dealing with a whole different type of scene. Or not dealing with it, as it happens.

Love,

Maggie.

For a long time Ellen refused to accept that her dad wasn't coming back. Robert threw tantrums, slammed doors, sulked and cried. Ellen did none of those things. She simply acted as if her dad was going through some minor mid-life crisis and would soon come to his senses.

The fact that he had moved in with his secretary was irrelevant as far as Ellen was concerned.

'He doesn't belong with that bitch,' she claimed. 'He belongs at home, with Mum and Robert and me, and sooner or later he's going to realise it.'

I said nothing. It seemed pretty clear to me that Mr B had made his choice. Even Mrs B didn't seem to be making any effort to convince him to come home. For ages she didn't bother getting out of bed until long after Ellen and Robert had left for school. Ellen made Robert's sandwiches in the morning as well as her own and nagged him to get dressed and out the door on time.

In school, the teachers were extra nice to Ellen. They didn't call on her to answer questions, or complain about her staring out the window. Even Fuddy Duddy refrained from comment when Ellen said she hadn't done her homework.

Some of the kids weren't as nice though. Girls can be such bitches.

Dear Ellen,

The cafeteria had curried chips today. Your favourite. I thought of you as Nuala dumped a steaming portion on my plate.

Not that I need a reason to think of you.

Most days I eat lunch alone. I sit by the window if I can. I know it's not something you would ever have taken any notice of, but I like looking out at the school garden. From the kitchen window, Nuala scatters crumbs for the birds. If there aren't too many first years running around screaming, or teachers coming and going in their cars, quite a lot of birds can gather just outside the window. Today I counted seven of them – one robin, and six little brown ones, which may have been starlings – I'm not sure. The robin was braver, swooping in straight away to get the best of the crumbs. The little brown birds held back a bit, waiting their turn, hopping cautiously forward when it looked like the coast was clear. I imagined them weighing things up – the tastiness of the crumbs, the distance from the safety of the bushes, the likelihood of bigger birds suddenly moving in, the whereabouts of the caretaker's cat.

I didn't notice how long I'd been watching them until I took a forkful of curried chips and realised they were cold.

Love,

Maggie.

In the long corridor outside the science lab, we waited for Miss Clark to arrive. Some of the girls were sitting on their schoolbags, while others leaned against the corridor wall, chatting. Ellen and I were perched on the windowsill. I was trying to look over my chemistry notes. Ellen was swinging her legs and talking about something she'd watched on TV the night before, not caring that I wasn't paying attention.

Siobhan Brady was whispering with one of her friends, a rather sly-faced girl who called herself Jacci with two 'c's (never Jackie – that would have been far too ordinary).

'Did you know …' Siobhan said to Jacci, looking in our direction, 'that one in three Irish teenagers now comes from a one-parent family?'

'Doesn't surprise me,' Jacci said flippantly. 'I mean, you hear about these things all the time, don't you?'

I glanced at Ellen. She had stopped talking and was staring steadfastly at a poster on the notice board. The faintest tinge of red was creeping into her cheeks.

'I suppose some of them were probably single mums from the time the babies were born,' Siobhan mused.

'And there must be some where the dad has died or something,' chimed in Jacci. She had a nasty glint in her eye and was clearly enjoying Ellen's growing discomfort.

'Yes, it must be so sad for kids to lose a dad like that,' Siobhan said. 'What I really can't understand though is how a man could just walk out on his family.'

'I know. Such a selfish thing to do,' Jacci said, shaking her head.

'Girls, don't,' said Carrie softly. Some of the other girls had stopped talking to listen, and there were one or two uncomfortable glances in Ellen's direction.

Siobhan took absolutely no notice of Carrie. 'And to run off with his secretary – a girl half his age? What kind of man would do' something like that? Only a sad old loser who couldn't care less about his kids.'

A flash of bright red hair and navy uniform, and before I had even fully realised that Ellen was no longer sitting beside me, she was across the corridor. Siobhan Brady's head snapped back, fistfuls of long blonde hair grasped in Ellen's hands.

'You take that back!' Ellen hissed.

Siobhan was screaming, tears rolling down her cheeks. Jacci was trying to pull Ellen away, but Ellen shoved her away with a sharp elbow.

'GIRLS!' Miss Clark surveyed the scene in horror. 'What on earth is going on?'

Abruptly, Ellen released Siobhan, who staggered, whimpering, and held on to Jacci to regain her balance.

'Miss, she just attacked me!' Siobhan blurted out.

Ellen said nothing. She simply looked at Siobhan with a sort of cold contempt. Around us, the rest of the class were staring in shocked silence.

'For like, no reason!' Siobhan whined.

'Hardly no reason,' I snapped.

Miss Clark gave me a sharp look. 'What do you mean, Maggie?'

I hesitated, looking at Ellen. She seemed determined to remain stonily silent.

Miss Clark looked over and back from one of us to the other. She seemed to make a quick decision. 'Right. Ellen, Maggie, Siobhan, Jacci. Into the science lab please. The rest of you, wait here until I call you. And not another word out of any of you!'

I picked up my bag and made my way into the lab, Ellen

beside me. Siobhan and Jacci followed, Siobhan still clutching her head and wearing a martyr-like expression.

The lab was all set up for our chemistry experiment. Bunsen burners stood in orderly rows on the benches, and the screen was set up behind Miss Clark's desk for the presentation. An unpleasant chemical smell lingered, left over from some earlier class's work.

Miss Clark lowered her pile of books and papers onto her desk and turned to look at us.

'Well?' she said. 'Would someone like to tell me what this is about?'

I stared at the ground. *Don't pick me*, I prayed silently.

'Ellen! Perhaps you could enlighten me as to why you felt it necessary to pull Siobhan's hair. That's the type of behaviour I'd expect from a two-year-old angry at someone for stealing her crayons.'

Her tone was so scathing I winced for Ellen. Ellen continued to say nothing.

Miss Clark waited. The silence grew until it seemed to fill the lab. There was no sound from the rest of the class, waiting outside in the corridor. Either they were scared into silence by Miss Clark's warning, or (more likely) they were straining to hear what was going on.

'Siobhan!' Miss Clark turned to her. 'Can you throw any light on the subject?'

'No, miss,' Siobhan said eagerly. 'Jacci and I were just talking about the chemistry experiment, and Ellen just attacked me for no reason.'

I saw Miss Clark's eyebrows go up at the first part of Siobhan's sentence. She was no fool. Typical of Siobhan, I thought scornfully, to go too far with her Good Little Schoolgirl act.

I wondered why Ellen didn't say anything, and whether I should speak up on her behalf.

'Well, Ellen?' Miss Clark said. 'Is this true? Did you perhaps have a difference of opinion with Siobhan about how best to conduct the experiment?'

Her sarcasm seemed to have the desired effect on Ellen, who finally spoke, though in a barely audible tone. 'No, miss.'

'Then why did you pull her hair?'

Silence again. The ticking of the clock above the whiteboard suddenly seemed almost ominously loud.

Miss Clark brought her hand down with a thump on her desk, making us all jump. 'Come on, girls! I'm going to get to the bottom of this even if it means standing here for the rest of the day.'

She meant it too. I watched the second hand on the clock slowly ticking by. Out of the corner of my eye I could see Siobhan and Jacci grimacing at each other. Any minute now Siobhan would start moaning, 'It's not *fair* ...'

'It wasn't Ellen's fault, miss!'

I think I was the one who was most surprised to hear me speak. Ellen looked at me, a warning on her face.

'Siobhan and Jacci were saying things about me ... saying my hair was horrible,' I said, blurting out the first thing that came into my head. 'Ellen was just sticking up for me.'

The look on Ellen's face changed to one of gratitude, and she surreptitiously squeezed my hand.

Miss Clark still looked suspicious. 'Siobhan – Jacci – is this true?'

'Yes, miss,' Siobhan muttered – much to my relief. For once in her life she'd had a bit of sense and realised that my lie was better than the truth.

Miss Clark sighed. 'Really, girls, this is not the type of behaviour I would expect from young ladies of your age!' She too seemed relieved that the little stand-off was over. She made her ruling. 'I'll see you in detention tomorrow evening – Siobhan, Jacci and Ellen that is. Maggie, your part in this has clearly been minimal.'

I thought to myself that detention would have been better than the last ten minutes of tortuous silence. Siobhan and Jacci said nothing, probably glad to have got off relatively lightly. Ellen certainly had. Detention was nothing to her. By the time Miss Clark had called the rest of the class in and we were all in our seats, she had got some of the sparkle back in her eye and was giving a whispered update to the girl on her other side. But Siobhan had clearly touched a nerve.

Dear Ellen,

Will this week ever end? I spent most of maths class looking at the clock. I wondered if it was really possible for the second hand to move around the clock so slowly. Every second was just endless. And then it was time for French, and I started the countdown all over again. Just one more class until break time. Just two more classes until lunch. Just three more classes until I can go home, and start my homework, and count down the hours until bedtime. And then I can start waiting for the next day to begin. Is this my life from now on?

I can't believe what a different place school is without you. Duller, greyer, lonelier. Not quieter though, like I would have expected. In fact some days I can't bear the noise. I feel like it's crowding in on me, and I can't hear my own thoughts any more.

Love, Maggie.

'Mum, can we go shopping after school?' Ellen asked. 'I need something to wear to the disco on Friday.'

Mrs B was having one of her Good Days and driving all four of us to school. I was stuck in the back between Jamie and Robert while Ellen sat up front with her mum.

'I don't think so, Ellen,' Mrs B said. 'What about that black top you got at Christmas? And your nice jeans?'

'Oh Mum, black is so last season! I don't want people thinking I'm some sort of a Goth!'

'What's a Goth?' Jamie wanted to know.

Mrs B kept her eyes firmly on the road. 'Well, there's your blue one with the sparkles.'

'I wore that the last time! Mum, you don't understand! I absolutely can't show my face at school on Monday if I have to wear that same old outfit again!' she declared, swooning back in her seat and sighing.

'What's a Goth?' repeated Jamie.

'I think it's some kind of a monster,' Robert whispered across me. I resisted the urge to giggle.

'Come on, Mum, will you get me something new?' Ellen demanded.

'A big black one, with huge black eyes?' Jamie suggested.

'Yeah, it's black so that it can hide in the dark. It follows you home at night and hides in your bedroom then pops out to gobble you up,' Robert said.

Jamie was starting to look a little bit scared. Robert is two years older than him and sometimes I think Jamie believes every word that he says, no matter how ridiculous. Normally I'd have stepped in to reassure Jamie but I was glued to the conversation in the front seat, wanting and not wanting to see what would happen next.

'Just a new top then,' Ellen bargained. 'I can wear the same jeans again if I really have to.'

'I am NOT discussing this now,' Mrs B said.

'But Mum, it's not like I'm asking for a whole new outfit,

or new boots, or a hundred quid to get my hair coloured or something! I just want a new top, is that really too much to ask?'

'We'll talk about it later,' said Mrs B. Her voice was starting to wobble a bit.

Shut up Ellen, I thought to myself. Last thing we needed was Mrs B getting all worked up.

Ellen either didn't notice or didn't care. 'But what do you think? Just a top?'

'Ellen, I am trying to concentrate on the road!' Mrs B snapped.

'Well, just answer me, then I'll stop bugging you!' said Ellen.

I could feel my face turning red. My mother would go mad if I spoke to her like that. Even Jamie and Robert were starting to squirm a bit, the monster debate forgotten.

'Come *on* Mum—

All of a sudden there was a screech of brakes as Mrs B stopped the car, right in the middle of the road. The boys and I were all jerked forwards in our seats. Cars behind us started honking their horns, and a cyclist shook his fist at us as he went past. Even Ellen looked a little shocked at what she had done.

Mrs B had gone all red in the face and her eyes were starting to water. 'All right, Ellen, I'll answer you. The answer is NO! You do NOT need new clothes – I am NOT buying you something just because you want it. In case you haven't noticed I am trying to bring up two children on my own since your father ran off with his little tart, and trying to make ends meet on the pittance he gives us every month! There are things we need a lot more urgently than a bloody new top for a girl who has a wardrobe bursting with clothes! Now I am NOT discussing this any further!'

Her voice kept getting screechier – by the end she was almost supersonic. Two fat tears trickled down her face.

'Oh fine, fine!' Ellen said.

Mrs B still didn't move. The honking from the cars behind us seemed to be getting even angrier.

'Is there any chance you could actually bring us to school now?' Ellen said sarcastically.

Mrs B said nothing, but she started the engine and drove off, looking straight ahead.

Ellen stared out the window sulkily, but by the time we reached the school gate she had cheered up. She slammed the car door, ignoring her mum's 'Goodbye!' and grabbed my arm.

'I've got a plan,' she whispered.

Dear Ellen,

Saturday – THANK GOD. No running around the all-weather pitch, no gagging at the sight of Fuddy Duddy's clothes, no conjugating French verbs or making up silly sentences about how many people there are in my family. Dad says he wants me to help him in the garden later, weeding and stuff. Apart from that I'm free all day. I think I will go shopping and see if they have those new boots in Ozzie's. Not that I can afford them, but I can lean against the window and sigh in admiration, and work out how many times I'd have to weed the garden to earn enough money to pay for them. How fast do weeds grow? Hmmm, not fast enough I suspect. Why on earth did I let you talk me into spending my birthday money on those hipster jeans? They don't even suit me, I don't know if my waist is too small or my hips are too big or what. Yours are perfect on you. Everything is.

I wonder if you ever got the purple boots you wanted. You would never have changed your mind and got the sensible black ones, would you?

Maybe I can earn the money some other way. I could do some typing for Aunt Pat, or walk the neighbour's dog. Or babysit those snotty kids in no. 22. Urgh. But it would all be worthwhile for a pair of the boots that KISS are calling THE must-have fashion item of the season.

I can't concentrate on my letter today. Jamie is being a total pest, kicking his ball against my bedroom door. I'm so tempted to yell at him but I'm trying to stay in Mum's good books. Maybe she will give me something towards the boots if I'm really good all weekend. You never know, it might be worth a try. God, he is really starting to annoy me though.

Now he's shouting something about Ireland winning the league. Ireland aren't in a league, you moron.

Oh good, Mum's shouting at him to 'come downstairs and leave Maggie in peace'. Excellent. Maybe she thinks I'm doing my homework.

I wonder what you are doing now. I wish I could talk to you. No one else really seems to understand. People are kind but they don't know what to say to me and I'm tired of being treated as some sort of freak show. And if anyone does try to ask me stuff I never know if it's because they actually care or if they just want to find out something about you so they can gossip about it.

I can hear Mum coming upstairs, so I'm going to put this away now as I don't want her to see it. I'll write again soon.

Love,

Maggie.

Ellen being Ellen, she got her own way in the end. Two days later she arrived into school with a shopping bag stuffed inside her schoolbag. She kept trying to show me what was in it during maths but Bouncer was too on the spot.

At break time she finally got her chance. She dragged me into the toilets and made straight for the mirrors, ignoring the crowd of girls milling around. She took out the shopping bag, and, almost with the air of a magician performing a trick, produced some gorgeous new jeans and not one but three new tops.

'What do you think?' She held the tops up in turn, admiring her reflection in the mirror.

'They're gorgeous. How on earth did you talk your mum into it?' I couldn't help being a little envious. I'd be wearing my same old black top that I'd worn a few months earlier, Goth-like or not. I wondered if I could do anything with it, sew some sequins on it or something.

'I didn't,' Ellen grinned. 'Dad took us out after school yesterday so I asked him to take us shopping. He was a bit reluctant but I just said I bet you take The Homewrecker shopping any time she wants. Although I didn't call her that to his face of course.'

She held the purple top up against me. 'This would be fab on you Maggie, why don't you borrow it? I think I'll wear the green one.'

'Oh I couldn't, you haven't even worn it yet,' I protested.

'Doesn't matter! I'll wear it with different jewellery when it's my turn.'

Ellen practised holding all her hair on top of her head to see if it showed off the green top better. I fingered the purple top longingly. 'Are you sure you don't mind?'

'Course not. It's all yours!'

I held it up against me and looked at our two reflections in the mirror – Ellen with her striking red hair and green eyes that always looked like they were planning something. She'd had an extra hole punched in each ear, and was wearing four different earrings. And there was me, so dull and ordinary beside her – mousy brown hair, blue eyes, proper little schoolgirl expression. Not for the first time I wondered why she was friends with me when all the popular girls wanted her to be in their gang.

'Won't we look fab?' Ellen said.

'Absolutely. These are just perfect for the disco,' I said.

Ellen had a wicked gleam in her eye. 'Oh no. We couldn't waste these on the disco.'

Dear Ellen,

When Mum came in earlier she asked if I wanted to go into town. Something about it not being healthy to be cooped up in my room all day. You know what mothers are like. So I gave in (you have to just let them have their own way sometimes, don't you?) and let her bring me into town. At least it meant getting away from the future no. 1 Ireland striker and his self-obsessed running commentary.

Mum was being all cheery and talking about it being 'just us girls' and how nice it was to have a little shopping trip on our own, and how glad she was to have a daughter to share these things with, and not just boys like Aunt Pat. I played along and nodded and smiled, but I was wishing you were in the back seat so I could roll my eyes at you.

For the whole drive in and the walk from the car park to

Java Bay she was all merry and cheerful, bustling along, yapping on and on about golf and Aunt Pat's fortieth birthday party and Dad's new lawnmower and Jamie's football match tomorrow, blah blah blah. I couldn't get a word in edgeways, which was fine with me because there was nothing I wanted to say. Then we're sitting having lunch, and the waitress brings over tea for Mum, and pink lemonade for me with two straws as usual. And Mum sees the two straws and suddenly dissolves into tears. That's what it was like – not bursting into tears, that's too dramatic – her face started to crumble or melt or something, and she put her hand up to her forehead, but I could still see the tears leaking out from under her fingers, and the edges of her mouth all sort of droopy-looking. And her shoulders were sort of trembling a bit. Not those big heaving sobs you get when you're really, really upset, just like she was trying very hard to stay still but somehow her body didn't want to. I didn't know what to say. There was nothing to say. She's my mother, she's the one who's supposed to be looking after me. So I just sipped my pink lemonade with one of the straws and stared at the table, wondering if all those shortbread crumbs were ours or if they just hadn't cleared the table after the last customers. The waitress came tiptoeing over and put a concerned hand on Mum's shoulder and held a wad of napkins out to her. Mum pressed the napkins to her nose and took a couple of deep breaths like she was trying to calm down.

People were staring at us at this stage. I didn't look around but I could feel their eyes on us, you know how you just know you are being watched. I said 'Oh do pull yourself together Mum' in my best Malory Towers voice, and took another slurp of my pink lemonade. Mum and the waitress laughed, the waitress uncertainly, as if she wasn't really sure if I was making a joke or not, and Mum in a sort of trembly, trying-to-be-strong way, like she did when she told me I needed my tonsils out and I asked if I could live on ice cream for a week.

I think Mum finally realised people were looking at us, because she started gulping down her tea and told me to finish my lemonade. I tried, but you know how big those glasses are, and suddenly there was an enormous lump in my throat which even pink lemonade couldn't seem to shift. She put on her cheerful voice again (slightly more shaky this time) and hurried me out of the cafe and off in the direction of Ozzie's.

I didn't even realise she knew about the boots, but there she was asking the assistant if they had the black ones in yet. The assistant said they did, and asked Mum if they were for her or her little sister. Mum did her tinkly little laugh and said that I was her daughter. (Like the assistant didn't know that. She probably thought if she flattered Mum enough she would buy matching pairs for the two of us – urgh, can you imagine?)

Mum told her my size and the girl produced a pair from the

stock room. They were every bit as nice as in the magazine –
enough of a heel to give me a bit of extra height, but not so
much as to have Dad tut-tutting about not having any daughter of his going out dressed like a tramp. (I always pretend
to misunderstand him when he says things like that, and
say that I thought tramps wore patchy old clothes, and bat-
tered hats, and shoes with holes in them, tied up with string
instead of laces. Drives him mad, and he mutters 'You know
very well what I mean young lady').

Anyway. The boots were gorgeous, though I suddenly
decided I wanted the purple ones. Mum said she thought I
wanted the black ones because they'd go with more stuff, but
I said no, it was definitely the purple I wanted. So she got the
girl to bring out a pair of the purple ones and I tried them
on. Perfect. But the lump in my throat was somehow getting
bigger, and I could only nod when Mum asked if I was happy
with them. I wandered off to look at some of the children's
shoes, trying hard to focus on the pink flowery ones with
little straps across the front, the kind we would have begged
our mums to buy when we were about six and really uncool.
Out of the corner of my eye I could see the girl wrapping up
the boots and ringing it up on the till, and Mum handing
over her laser card – €120, just like that. I tried a little boy's
runner on my hand and made it walk along the shelf so the
lights lit up at the back, little flashes of red. Mum came over
with the boots in a big box inside a bag, and said something

about the box coming in handy for storing my art stuff. I put the runner back, wondering if they made them with different coloured lights, or was it always red. Mum asked if I'd rather carry the boots myself, but I shook my head, and we left the shop and walked back towards the car.

I'm wearing the boots now. I can see them in the mirror at the end of my bed. They're lovely, and you were right, they are much cooler than the black, and who cares about being practical? But somehow the excitement is gone. It's an anti-climax or something. They're just boots after all.

Your friend,

Maggie.

The bell was ringing for the end of break but I ignored it. 'What do you mean?' I asked her, half excited, half nervous.

'Just look at us!' Ellen said, preening in front of the mirror. 'We look fabulous. At least seventeen. I bet we could pass for eighteen with make-up on. How could we waste this on a silly teen disco we've been to thousands of times before?'

'But what else is there?' I realised I sounded stupid, but I really didn't know what Ellen had in mind.

She pulled a poster out of her schoolbag. 'I took this from a noticeboard in town. There's a band playing in a pub just down the road from the disco. Flaming Moes, have you heard of them? They're fantastic.' She started humming some song I'd never heard of.

'Sounds cool,' I said, taking the poster out of her hand. 'But there's no way my parents would let me go to a pub. There's no point in even asking.'

Ellen laughed. 'Who said anything about asking? We'll just get one of our mums to drop us at the disco as usual. We'll go in the front door and straight out the back door and down to the pub. Easy peasy. We can be back at the disco again before it's over.'

I didn't say anything. I wasn't sure I liked the sound of this. I didn't like lying to my mum. And I was the kind of person who always ended up getting caught. Plus, sad though it was, I was actually looking forward to the disco – especially if I could wear Ellen's new purple top. The disco was on every couple of weeks in the tennis club near the school, and was a strictly no alcohol zone. Liam would be there, and his friends of course. Ellen had said she thought one of his friends liked me. I didn't know which one but thought that I might find out at the disco.

Ellen sensed my hesitation. 'Oh come on, Maggie, say you'll come! They're such a cool band, I know you'll like them.'

'I'm not sure. What if we don't get in? What if someone notices we're not at the disco and asks our mums where we were? What if there's someone we know at the pub? What if …?' I trailed off. I think I'd run out of disasters.

'Maggie you are such a worrier,' Ellen laughed. 'Live dangerously for once! *Carpe diem* and all that. What's the worst thing that can happen?'

The corridor outside was quiet. Everyone must be back in their classrooms by now. If we didn't hurry we'd be late for geography.

I didn't want to be a party pooper. 'OK then,' I said, 'if you really want to.'

'Excellent! It'll be fab, I promise! Now hurry up, I don't want you to start giving out that I made you late for geography!' Ellen grabbed my hand and rushed me out of the bathroom just as she'd rushed me in ten minutes earlier, stuffing the tops back into her bag any old way as she went. Now they'd need to be ironed before we could wear them. Oh well.

Dear Ellen,

Sunday afternoon. I'm supposed to be doing my maths homework. But these triangles and trapeziums and so on aren't making any sense to me. My mind is like one of those scribbles Jamie used to do at playschool and Mum would proudly stick to the fridge – a jumble of lines and colours, all going in different directions and doubling back on themselves – and I can't make any straight lines out of it.

Dad asked me to help with the weeding today. I thought I'd managed to get out of it when Mum took me into town yesterday, but no such luck. But once I got started I found I was enjoying it in a funny sort of way. Aunt Pat would say it was therapeutic. I liked the repetitiveness of pulling up the weeds and chucking them into the wheelbarrow. Pull, throw, pull, throw. And I liked looking back at the section I'd just finished, seeing the flowers sort of standing up proudly in a nice clean patch, not competing for space with all those weeds trying to choke them.

But then Dad had to go and ruin it. He pushed his glasses back on his nose (always a danger sign) and said he thought it was about time we had a little chat. I tried to discourage him by just ignoring him, concentrating hard on a particularly stubborn bit of dandelion root that was trying to choke the pansies. He started saying something about there being a natural process to go through, and it not being a good idea to bottle things up, and so on. That was when I suddenly remembered I hadn't finished my maths homework, and had to go inside.

I think Dad fancies himself as some sort of amateur psychologist. Well, he can try his theories out on Jamie if he must. I'd like to see him unravel the mystery of how a little boy's brain works, and why he thinks vegetables are disgusting, but cutting worms in half with a stone is fun.

You're the only person I'd really like to talk to about all this – but then, if you were here, there'd be nothing to talk about, would there?

Your friend, Maggie.

As the week went on I got more and more nervous about Friday night. I couldn't stop thinking about all the things that could go wrong.

The thing was, I just wasn't the type of person who did things like that. It's like I was missing the teenage rebellion gene or something. But Ellen had a double dose so I guess we always balanced each other out. Sometimes I used to wonder what someone like her could see in someone like me. Maybe she actually liked the fact that I could usually stop her before she did anything too crazy. Or at least I used to be able to.

Ellen was completely oblivious to my worrying. She laughed and chatted away as normal when the subject of the school disco came up, catching my eye and grinning when no one else was looking.

Her giddiness seemed to grow as the week went on. I'd seen her like this before − if she didn't find some kind of outlet for it, she might possibly explode.

Wednesday was April Fools' Day. It was just what Ellen needed. I'd already been treated to salt in my cornflakes instead of sugar by the ever-original Jamie, and Dad had told me there was something stuck to the bottom of my shoe, then fell about the place laughing when I took it off to check. Honestly, he is so juvenile sometimes.

Ellen's joke was, of course, a lot more imaginative. She whispered to me on our way into maths, 'How would you like to spend this class walking to and from the gym instead of adding x's and y's?'

'Sounds like a better option all right,' I whispered back. 'What have you got in mind?'

'Wait and see!' was Ellen's only response.

We had Bouncer for maths. He was a small man – half the girls in our class were already taller than him – and he attempted to make up for his lack of height by wearing these shoes with springy soles that made him look like he was bouncing every time he moved around the classroom. He was OK – a bit too earnest sometimes in expecting everyone to be as enthusiastic about algebra as he was – but not one of the worst.

Ellen waited until everyone was seated and Bouncer was just about to demonstrate a sum on the board, then waved her hand in the air.

'Sir! Sir! I've just remembered. Miss O'Neill said could you please excuse us from maths today. She wants us all in the gym. Something about basketball trials, I think.'

'I think you must have got that wrong Ellen,' Bouncer said dismissively. 'She must have meant during PE this afternoon.'

'Oh no, sir,' Ellen said confidently. 'She specifically said it had to be this morning. Apparently it's very urgent. Actually she said she would ask you herself but she obviously ran out of time or something.'

She was looking at him with such innocent wide green

eyes, I had to put my hand over my mouth to stop myself from giggling.

Bouncer looked annoyed. 'We have quite a lot of work to do today, I really can't see why a basketball trial should be more important than that.'

'Do you want me to go and find her, sir?' Ellen suggested. She was probably thinking that at least she'd get a few minutes out of class even if she wasn't going to manage to get us all out with her fairly ambitious scam.

'Yes, please do. As quickly as you can,' the teacher said. 'Now everyone, open your books at page 53.'

Ellen made a big deal of scraping back her chair and picking up a tissue from the floor, taking the opportunity to whisper to me 'Bet I can get old O'Neill to go along with it! Lunch is on you if I'm right!'

Then she was gone, banging the door behind her in her usual subtle way.

Dear Ellen,

When the guards were asking me about you, it was so hard to know what to say. I wanted to be helpful, but telling them too much personal stuff just felt like a betrayal. They were very focused on your state of mind. Isn't that a funny phrase? State of mind – as if that was something I would ever be able to describe to them with something as elusive and slippery as words. They tried putting words on it for me. Angry. Frightened. Mixed up. Out of control. You were all those things, and yet you were happy too, most of the time, this kind of exhilarating buzz which was sometimes completely infectious and sometimes just plain annoying. And underneath, I know you were just this scared kid who'd had to grow up much too fast and really wanted someone just to hold you and tell you everything was going to be OK.

I talked to that nice guard Declan – remember? From the cinema night? – a few times. Well, mostly he talked, and I just listened, because there wasn't much I could say that would have been any help.

Sometimes it feels like I'm the one who's missing, like I'm not really present in my own life any more – I'm like a ghost or something, wandering through school or home or town looking on at everything that's happening and not really a part of it at all.

Love,

Maggie.

I waited, wondering how on earth Ellen thought she could convince the hearty and loud-voiced Miss O'Neill to play a joke on a fellow teacher. She had never struck me as being possessed of much of a sense of humour, her two main passions in life being exercise and fresh air.

Ellen was gone for a good ten minutes. I began to suspect that she'd been unable to convince Miss O'Neill. She had probably just decided to take the long way back to miss as much algebra as possible. Then, just when I was finally getting my head around the sum Bouncer was trying to explain, the door opened and a triumphant Ellen marched in, followed by an unexpected figure – not Miss O'Neill, but our very grand principal Mrs Carmichael!

'I'm so sorry to interrupt your class,' she said politely, 'but I'm afraid Miss O'Neill needs the girls in the gym. The basketball trials are terribly urgent as we are playing St Luke's next week, and the entire school's honour is at stake.'

'Of course, of course,' Bouncer blustered, clearly taken aback at the arrival of the principal. 'Right girls, pack up your bags and off you go.'

I stared in amazement at Ellen. How on earth had she managed to pull that one off? As Mrs Carmichael left I saw her give Ellen a little wink and could hardly believe it. Our usual staid and sensible principal was actually helping perpetrate an April Fools' Joke and making us miss maths!

Ellen arrived back at my side. 'Java Bay for lunch then, Maggie?' she suggested with a grin. 'I quite fancy a nice chicken wrap, I think, and maybe a strawberry smoothie to go with it.'

'What happened? How did you convince her?' I demanded, shoving my maths book into my bag. Bouncer was barking orders, hurrying people along, obviously not wanting to delay the basketball trials any further.

We made our way to the door.

'It was easy,' Ellen giggled. 'I thought Miss O'Neill would be in the staff room so I went there, I was planning on trying to persuade her to go along with the joke. But Mrs Carmichael came to the door and said O'Neill wasn't there, so I decided I'd ask her instead – I figured what's the worst thing that could happen?'

'Eh, she could eat you alive?' I said.

'Well, she didn't,' said Ellen, unperturbed.

Some of the other girls were crowding around now, demanding to know what was going on.

'Are there really basketball trials?' Niamh asked.

'There can't be, it's some kind of April Fool right?' said someone else.

''Fraid so, ladies. So sorry to make you miss maths,' Ellen said. 'But I wasn't really in the mood for quadratic equations.'

'Thank goodness for that!' Carrie said. 'I didn't have my homework done, I was just waiting for Bouncer to have a go at me.'

'So what happened?' Niamh demanded. 'What did you say to Mrs Carmichael?'

Ellen looked back to check if Bouncer was following, but he had gone, bouncing off in the direction of the staff room.

'I just explained we wanted to play a little April Fool on Bouncer,' she said airily. 'Mrs Carmichael just smiled and said she'd go along with it. Apparently the staff were planning an

April Fool of their own on Bouncer. She said I'd given her a great excuse to get him off to the staff room!'

'You nutter! Only you would get away with something like that,' Niamh said.

'Come on, we'd better go,' Ellen said. 'Carmichael said we have to walk to the gym and then go on to our next class, so I suppose we'd better do it. Race you there!'

Dear Ellen,

Another Monday, another detention. Yep, Bouncer put me in detention for not having my maths homework done. I tried to explain about the wavy lines but he wouldn't listen. Looks like 'Be nice to Maggie week' is well and truly over. Same with Mum this morning. She wouldn't let me wear my new boots to school. Something about them being unsuitable and against the school code.

Siobhan Brady was in detention too. She told me proudly that she'd managed to tick two names off her list over the weekend. Sean O'Connor at the cinema on Friday night, and James Doherty at a party on Saturday. Lucky them.

Sometimes when I'm on my way to school I imagine you're going to be there, putting books in your locker and chatting at a million miles an hour, as if nothing had happened. I keep hoping that if I picture it hard enough, it might actually come true.

Your friend,

Maggie.

When we got to the school gate Liam was waiting, leaning against the pillar with his phone in his hand, his school bag and football gear in a heap at his feet. I couldn't help noticing the way his dark hair fell to the top of his collar – just about within the regulation length for the boys' school.

Liam has known Ellen even longer than I have. He lives next door to her and their mums have been friends since Liam and Ellen were babies.

Mrs B likes to tease Ellen about how she and Liam used to run around the garden together in the nip when they were toddlers, jumping in and out of the paddling pool and splashing each other. Ellen just rolls her eyes and changes the subject. If it was me I'd be mortified. I hate those kind of stories.

His face lit up when he saw us coming. When he saw Ellen coming, I mean.

'Didn't see you in the Four Lights today,' he remarked, referring to the fast food place which was our usual place to go when we needed to escape the canteen.

'Actually, Maggie treated me to lunch in Java Bay,' Ellen said.

'Yes – not that I actually agreed to the bet in the first place,' I said.

'What bet was this then?' Liam asked. 'Anything to do with the Champions League match last night?'

'As if!' Ellen scoffed. She filled him in on the April Fools'

51

joke. It gave me a funny feeling in my stomach the way he hung on her every word.

'Can't believe your principal went along with that,' Liam said, the admiration clear in his voice.

Ellen laughed. 'Oh it was just a lucky coincidence that the teachers had something of their own planned. Wish I'd been there to see that one!'

I know it wasn't very nice of me, but I was getting a bit tired of hearing about Ellen's fabulous joke. First Mrs Carmichael going along with it, then the other girls thronging around her like a bunch of groupies. And now Liam.

'Are you working this weekend?' I asked him, trying to change the subject. Liam had a part-time job in his parents' newsagents shop. I'd often seen him there at weekends, lugging boxes around, stacking shelves, stopping to chat to old ladies or toddlers clinging on to their mums' hands. He even seemed to enjoy being in charge of the ice cream machine, swirling the soft white ice cream onto the cone, so high it looked like it would topple over any second. Jamie was a sucker for those cones. Mum often bribed him with one if he behaved himself in Tesco.

'I might do a few hours on Saturday afternoon,' Liam said. 'Only if they're stuck though. Got a fair bit of studying to do.'

'Not in the morning then?' I asked. It was usually on Saturday mornings that Mum dragged me off to the shopping centre, wanting me to trail along behind her like a little kid while she tried on clothes or looked for a birthday present for someone.

'No, I've got a match on Saturday morning,' said Liam. 'You should come!' He looked at Ellen as he said this, and again I felt that strange pang.

'Thanks but I reckon we'll be too tired after Friday night,' said Ellen.

'Oh, you're going to the disco then?' Liam said eagerly. 'Should be a good night.'

'Yeah, we're really looking forward to it, aren't we, Maggie?' Ellen said, nudging me. 'Wouldn't miss it for the world!'

'Great! Do you need a lift?' Liam asked, doing his best to look nonchalant, but I could see he was practically holding his breath waiting for Ellen's reply. 'I mean, my mum has her bridge night anyway, she could drop us off on the way. You too, of course, Maggie,' he added.

I could hardly look at him. He was so eager and yet trying to act cool, and we weren't even going to be there.

'Oh it's OK,' Ellen said hastily. 'I'm staying over at Maggie's that night so we'll probably just get ready at her place. See you there though, OK?'

'Sure. See you then!'

'So, looks like I'm staying at your place then!' Ellen giggled as we walked away. 'You don't mind do you?'

'No, of course not. I was going to suggest it anyway,' I said. This was true. My mother was always slightly anxious when I was going out, and with Mrs B being so unpredictable at the moment I think she didn't really trust her to pick us up when she said she would.

'Great! We can pool our make-up and see what works best with our new tops. I was thinking green shimmer with mine, what do you reckon?'

'Mmmm … sounds nice.'

I glanced back at Liam. I felt so sorry for him. Couldn't Ellen see how much he liked her?

Dear Ellen,

I saw Liam today at lunchtime. He was sitting in the square on his own, just texting on his phone. He reminded me a bit of Heathcliff actually, all sort of brooding and melancholy. If you can imagine Heathcliff in a school uniform, and holding a mobile phone that is.

I wanted to go over and talk to him, but I felt a bit funny about it. I know he's missing you too.

Some days I feel like I just can't wait to get out of here. I think of the two of us at college, sharing a flat, where there's no one to check up on us or ask us endless questions about where we're going and what time we'll be home.

Where we're going, of course, is to parties, and concerts, and on double dates with strings of unsuitable men. And the next day we'll sit around outside cafes drinking black coffee and laughing our heads off about these guys, and everything else. And maybe, eventually, when the right one comes along, falling in love.

We might go to the occasional lecture too, of course, if it doesn't interfere with our social lives too much. And at weekends I'll drag you along to car boot sales to look for vintage tea dresses and faux pearl necklaces, and you can drag me along to gigs in cellar bars where we sit at high stools and drink cocktails while watching the band.

Liam keeps popping up in these daydreams too, though I can't quite work out how he fits in. He's just there, helping himself to cups of tea in our flat, or sitting beside us in a lecture, or hanging around in the background at one of the parties, making sure we're both OK.

You will be back by then Ellen, won't you? I'm keeping this notebook safe for you because I want to believe you'll read it some day, and you'll know I never stopped hoping you'd come home.

Love,

Maggie.

My dad decided to do a barbecue on the night of the disco. Mum invited Robert over to play with Jamie and stay the night along with Ellen. I knew she wanted to give Mrs B a break. She even went over to collect them.

Ellen was barely out of the car before she started. 'Let's start getting ready right away. We need to see what eye shadow works best!'

'Don't you think you should wait until after dinner?' Mum said to me. 'You don't want to spill something on your party dress.'

Is she ever going to stop embarrassing me like this? Are mums genetically programmed to embarrass you and treat you like a little kid? 'Oh Mum, I'm not going to spill something. And I'm not wearing a *party dress*! Stop treating me like I'm five years old.'

Mum relented. 'Go on then, the two of you may as well start getting ready. Off you go upstairs. Boys, you can go outside and play football until dinner's ready.'

'Come on, Maggie, let's get you into your flowery dress, or is it your pink frilly one?' Ellen teased me as we went upstairs. 'And then I can put your hair in two plaits for you if you like!'

'Stop it – it's bad enough her doing it,' I grumbled. 'She's driving me crazy with questions about the disco, who's going to be there, what time will it be over, blah blah blah! Honestly I wish she'd just leave me alone.'

'At least she cares about you,' Ellen said, a funny hard tone in her voice. 'I don't think my mum even gets that there's a disco on.'

I stared at her. 'Sorry, Ellen, I didn't mean ... I'm sure your mum ...' I trailed off.

Ellen was rummaging in her bag, her back to me. 'Look, here's my purple sparkly eye shadow,' she said. 'Try it on.'

'Are you OK?' I asked.

'Why wouldn't I be? I'm young, free and single, I have new clothes and a gig to wear them to!' She spun around the room, tossing me her purple top and holding the green one up again herself.

'Are you sure you don't mind me wearing the top?' I asked for the fifteenth time. I felt bad about borrowing something Ellen hadn't even worn yet. Knowing Siobhan Brady she'd probably notice the next time Ellen wore it and use it as yet another thing to taunt her with.

'Course I don't mind. I want to wear the green one anyway. Brings out the colour of my eyes,' Ellen said, applying mascara to her long lashes.

Through the open window I could hear the boys shouting, another game of football underway, and Dad humming a Beatles song out of tune as he flipped burgers. They smelled delicious and I could feel my stomach growling.

I put on the purple top. It really was nice. I twisted from side to side in front of the mirror, admiring it.

'Ellen! Ellen!'

Robert was shouting from the garden.

Ellen leaned out the window. 'What is it?'

'Come and play football with us!'

I was about to tell him to get lost, but Ellen said 'OK, just give us a minute!'

I groaned. 'Not football again!'

'Oh come on, we can give them a few minutes, it's not much of a game with only one on each team!'

I dabbed at the purple eye shadow. Were the sparkles just a bit too sparkly? I didn't want to look overdone.

'Have you not finished beautifying yourself yet?' Ellen demanded. 'Come on, you're gorgeous! Let's go and give them a quick game before the barbecue's ready. I'll even let you go in goal!'

I followed her downstairs and out to the garden. It really wasn't warm enough for a barbecue yet, but my dad always takes it out at the first sign of sun. He just loves the image of himself as a chef, standing at the barbecue in his blue and white stripy apron, preparing macho food for his family. Cooking normal food indoors is clearly not the same.

'Come on then, who's on my team?' Ellen demanded.

'You're not playing football in those sandals, are you?' my mum asked, smiling.

'Nope!' Ellen kicked them off and ran onto the grass in her bare feet. 'Right, Robert, you're with me. Jamie, come and play, Maggie's going to go in goal.'

Soon she was running about like a loon, not caring that her carefully styled hair was getting all messed up. I'm not really a fan of football, but I couldn't help enjoying myself, her mood was as infectious as ever.

'Food's ready!' Dad called.

We all trooped over to the picnic table, red-faced and tired. My mum shivered, pulling her cardigan closer. 'I really think it's a bit early to be eating in the garden. Don't you think we should go indoors?'

'Of course not!' said Dad, shocked. 'It's not a barbecue if you eat it indoors. Put on another layer. Here, you can have my fleece.' He wrapped it carefully around her shoulders and she smiled up at him. He gave her one of those lovey-dovey looks which used to embarrass the hell out of me, but which I now think are kind of sweet.

I saw Ellen gazing at them, that hard look beginning to creep into her face again.

'So chef, what's on the menu tonight?' I said hastily.

'Oooh, Ballymaloe relish instead of ketchup,' Ellen said. 'Aren't we posh!'

'Oh, it's not just the relish,' I said. 'We have homemade chips and everything.'

'No frozen chips in my house!' Dad said. 'They're an abomination. Give me homemade chips any day. Although a trip to the chipper for an occasional treat is fine by me.'

'Well, let's get it into us! No time to waste, the disco awaits!' Ellen said.

'What's up with you two this evening?' my mother asked with a laugh. 'You're wound up. Anyone would think this was your first time at a disco!'

Ellen laughed. 'Not really, but somehow it feels like a first all the same!'

Mum dropped us off at the disco, reminding us about fourteen times that she would collect us at midnight.

Ellen grabbed my arm and marched me in the direction of the hall door, keeping an eye all the time on my mum's car. As soon as it turned the corner she changed direction, pulling me around the corner and out of sight of the parents dropping off their teenagers.

'Now!' she said.

Dear Ellen,

I've asked Mum to stop collecting me from school. It's not a very long walk home, only about forty-five minutes if I walk quickly. Maybe an hour if I dawdle. It makes a nice change, anyway. I don't have to go straight from Fuddy Duddy rab-bitting on to Mum asking questions and Jamie bouncing around in his booster seat pointing out every motorbike and tractor that we pass. I like to just walk and walk and not have to listen to anyone.

Some days I walk past the sweet factory. The air around it is filled with the smell of chocolate and orange, or strawberry, or mint. Sometimes it makes me think of the time we went on a school tour there. We were so excited to see the whole process of sweets being made, the machines and big vats, and all the noises and smells. It felt like we were in Willy Wonka's chocolate factory, and I half expected to see an Oompa Loompa peeping at me around a corner.

Other days, going past the sweet factory reminds me of their float in the St Patrick's Day parade. It was always our favourite. Every year they had a new theme, always something magical and full of bright colours, and the staff dressed up in their costumes would throw sweets to all the children in the crowd.

Sometimes I walk through the park. The leaves have all changed colour, reds and oranges and browns, and great mounds of them rise at the edge of the path, where the park keepers have swept them. I glance all around me to see if anyone's watching. If the coast is clear, I step off the path and kick my way through the leaves, liking the way they rise up before me and float back down to resettle somewhere else. When I get to the end I turn to look back. The piles are a little flatter, the leaves a little more scattered, but anyone looking at them for the first time wouldn't know that someone had just walked through them. There's no trace of me at all.

At first Mum wasn't very happy about me walking home alone. She raised all sorts of objections. What if it rained? What about my heavy schoolbag, how would I manage that? Wouldn't I be too tired to do my homework by the time I got home? I answered her quietly and calmly. It's my new technique. I find it's a far better way of getting what I want than arguing and screaming and slamming doors. She thinks I'm being rational and mature, when actually all I am being is sneaky in a new way.

Soon it will be getting darker earlier. I expect Mum will want to start collecting me again. She won't want me walking through the park after dark. So I'd better enjoy the silence while it lasts.

Love,

Maggie.

'We'll have to wait a few minutes,' Ellen said. 'Give everyone a chance to get in. We don't want someone's mum or dad seeing us and asking awkward questions.'

I peeped around the corner. Three cars were pulled up outside, boys and girls jumping out, parents shouting instructions and reminders about pick-up times. No sign of Liam – maybe he was already inside.

I rubbed my arms, feeling cold in Ellen's purple top. She had insisted that we leave our jackets at home, saying we didn't want the bother of looking after them. Though for some reason she'd brought a large shoulder bag with her – it was hot pink and made of straw, the kind of thing you'd bring to the beach for a day out, instead of her usual small glittery one that was just about big enough to hold a lip gloss and some money.

I soon found out the reason for the bag.

'Anyone watching?' she asked me, rooting around in the bag.

I checked again. 'No one near, everyone's heading straight in. A few more cars dropping people off. Siobhan Brady's wearing a ridiculous amount of eye shadow. She looks like she's got two black eyes.'

I turned around. Ellen had pulled a short black skirt over her jeans and was now wriggling out of the jeans underneath.

'Didn't think your mum would approve of this skirt!' she said. I didn't think so either. It barely covered her knickers.

She quickly shoved her jeans into the bag. She looked amazing. I wished I had the guts to wear a skirt like that.

'You look fab!' I said, trying to keep the envy out of my voice.

Ellen shrugged. She was so used to compliments she just took them in her stride.

'What's happening now?'

I peeped again. 'Still a few stragglers going in.'

The cold was really getting to me now. And I didn't know how Ellen could bear it – she wasn't even wearing any tights. Her feet were in silver sandals and she had painted her toe nails a deep cherry red. I thought of everyone gathering inside the club, taking up the usual positions – girls hanging around near the DJ, giggling behind their hands, surreptitiously pointing out a boy they think their friend fancies.

Boys joking, shoving each other and laughing; some of the quieter ones lurking at the sides, drinking cans of Coke and not talking to anyone. Glances exchanged across the room, catching someone's eye, holding their gaze just a fraction longer than necessary. Liam was probably chatting to his mates while keeping an eye on the door to make sure he saw Ellen as soon as she arrived.

Ellen leaned around me. 'Come on, let's risk it now!' she said. 'I can't see any parents or teachers – and none of those little first years would dare say anything to us!'

We walked briskly past the tennis club, not wanting to draw any attention by running – anyway Ellen's heels didn't look like they would stand too much running. Soon we were well out of sight of the hall. I began to relax a little. As Ellen liked to say, what's the worst that could happen?

Dear Ellen,

This evening, Liam was waiting as I came out of school, standing at the gate with his hands in his pockets. Neither of us spoke. He reached out to take my art folder and I let him. We walked through the town and when we came to the place where the road forks in two we both turned towards the park in silent agreement. I didn't kick the leaves. Everything was so still, so quiet, I didn't want to disturb the peace. Liam seemed to feel the same way because he just walked quietly beside me, swinging my art folder as he went. We came to my road and he turned down it with me, even though it's out of his way. And still neither of us said a word.

As we got to my house Liam handed me the folder and said, 'See you tomorrow then.' And then he was gone.

Love,

Maggie.

The pub was packed. Ellen elbowed her way through and I followed, clinging on to her bag so I wouldn't lose sight of her. She jostled someone's arm, spilling her drink, and the woman snapped 'Hey, look where you're going!'

'Sorry!' I gasped, pushing Ellen on before she could snap back at her.

One of the barmen, a young man with very short hair and a single earring, was following our progress across the bar. I tried to keep my head down, thinking he was working out how old we were. Then I realised that what was attracting his interest was Ellen's short skirt – or rather her long legs.

Finally Ellen found us some seats, a couple of low stools at the edge of someone else's table. She shoved aside someone's coat and sat down.

'Great, we've got a pretty good view of the band from here,' she said, waving her hand in the direction of the small platform where the band were beginning to set up. I noticed she seemed to be paying particular attention to one of them – a young guy of about nineteen or twenty dressed all in black, with slightly greasy-looking long hair tied back in a ponytail. Not my type, which meant he probably was Ellen's.

I couldn't stop feeling self-conscious. Ellen's purple top was a bit lower than I realised – I could see the edge of my white bra peeping out at the top. I tried to surreptitiously pull it down at the back.

I needed somewhere to put my hands. We weren't close enough to the table to hide them under there, and I was suddenly very aware of them just sitting there in my lap.

'I'll get us some drinks, will I?' I suggested. I wasn't exactly thrilled at the prospect of fighting my way to the bar, but at least we might blend in a bit better if we were sipping on drinks instead of just sitting there.

'Make mine a vodka and Coke!' Ellen responded.

I groaned inwardly. As if it wasn't bad enough that we had snuck off to a pub while our mums thought we were at the teen disco, now she wanted us to get caught drinking alcohol? I mean, my parents don't mind me having a glass of wine with dinner at home with them. Actually they sort of encourage it. They like to think they are being terribly cool and laidback. And they seem to think that if I can have it at home I won't feel the need to go to pubs or hang around with my friends outside off-licences, pooling our money and hoping someone will buy us some beer. So any time they're opening a bottle of wine for Sunday dinner or whatever, they'll pour me a small glass, and then tease me that I'm getting merry when I'm nothing of the sort.

But vodka? And in a pub where we shouldn't have been in the first place?

Ellen didn't seem to notice my reaction so I made my way to the bar, wondering what to do. Should I buy her a vodka and just get a Coke for myself? Should I stop being such a wimp and just get us both vodkas? One each couldn't hurt, could it? Would the barman even serve me?

A couple of girls of nineteen or twenty, looking very glamorous in glittering eye shadow and short dresses, let me squeeze in beside them at the bar. It was packed and stuffy and I was starting to be glad Ellen hadn't let me bring my jacket. Eventually the barman noticed me – the same one who hadn't been able to take his eyes off Ellen's long brown legs as we made our way in.

My courage deserted me. 'Two Cokes please,' I muttered. He brought me my order without comment and I scuttled back to Ellen, glad the ordeal was over.

She wasn't alone. The guy in black, who'd been setting up for the band, was sitting in my place. Ellen had edged closer to the table and was leaning her elbow on it, head resting on her hand as she giggled at something he was saying.

I cleared my throat.

'Oh Pete, this is my friend Maggie,' Ellen said. 'Maggie, this is Pete. He's with the band.'

The way she said it it might have been U2 he was with,

not some amateur pub band playing their fourth or fifth gig. I noticed his T-shirt had the name Flaming Moes printed on it, along with an ugly-looking skull and crossbones.

'Hi,' I said shyly.

Pete gave me a lazy smile. 'Maggie, is it? Wait till you see the band, they've been working on some new material and it's pretty damn good.'

He made no attempt to get out of my seat. I stood there awkwardly, still holding the Cokes. Ellen reached out to take one from me.

'Sorry, it's just Coke,' I said. 'The barman was asking for ID so I was afraid we'd get thrown out.' I blushed as I spoke. I've never been any good at lying.

'You can't listen to the Flaming Moes when you're drinking coke!' Pete said. 'I'll get you some proper drinks. Vodka, is it? Or Bacardi?'

'Vodka, please.' Ellen gave him her most engaging smile, the one she uses to wrap her dad around her little finger.

My heart sank. I couldn't make up another excuse now or I'd have to admit I lied about not getting served. Oh well, one vodka couldn't do much harm.

Pete started battling his way to the bar just as the band began their first song. Actually I don't think you could really call it a song, it was really just a lot of noise. Oh dear, I sound like my dad now, but I just can't bear music where the drums are so loud you can't even hear the words. The lyrics are the most important part of the song to me.

'This is brilliant!' Ellen screeched, bouncing up and down on her stool. Pete arrived back with the vodkas and Ellen tipped the Cokes into them, handing one to me. I sipped it cautiously, feeling the warmth spreading to my stomach. It felt quite good actually and I could feel myself starting to relax a little.

Dear Ellen,

After it happened your photo was all over the papers. The one of you at the seaside last summer, leaning against the railing at the top of the steps that led down to the beach. I couldn't believe it when I saw what photo your mum had given them, because I knew you hated that photo – you said your eyes looked small and weird. It was a blazing hot day and you were squinting in the sunlight as you looked into the camera. The sun was making your hair all glistening and coppery, and bits of it were blowing in your face – you had one hand up, about to brush them away, but the camera had caught you just a second before, so it looked like you might be waving. I thought it was an OK photo of you but there were so many nicer ones, I don't know why your mum picked that one, when she must have known you hated it. Then again, maybe she didn't. She wasn't exactly clued in to what you were thinking.

I couldn't have avoided seeing that photo, it was everywhere in those first weeks – so much so that I just don't understand how it was possible for you to remain lost.

Love,

Maggie.

Seven pieces of noise – sorry, songs – later, my ears were ringing, I was too hot, the flashing lights were getting to me and my head was starting to swim. Ellen was deep in conversation with Pete, though goodness knows how they were managing to understand each other. I'd given up trying to shout in Ellen's ear above the noise, it just wasn't worth the effort.

Liam would have given up on us by now. He might even have started talking to Siobhan Brady and her friends. Siobhan has always had a thing for Liam though she'd never admit it in front of Ellen. Ellen doesn't want Liam for herself but she doesn't want anyone else to have him either.

I glanced at my watch. It was five to twelve! The disco was finishing at midnight – Mum would probably be there waiting already.

I touched Ellen's arm. 'Ellen, we have to go!'

'What?!' she shouted.

I pointed to my watch. 'WE – HAVE – TO – GO!' I mouthed.

'Oh, come on, let's just stay for one more song! It won't matter if we're a few minutes late.'

'Not leaving already, are you? The night's just getting started. I was just starting to enjoy myself,' Pete said, sweeping his hand out in a gesture that might have meant the band, the entire pub, or just himself and Ellen.

Ellen was wavering. I thought of the one argument that might persuade her. 'If we get caught we'll be grounded for weeks. There's no way we'll get to see the next gig,' I said urgently.

'What's the matter, are you some kind of Cinderella? Afraid you'll turn into a pumpkin at midnight?' Pete laughed at his own pathetic joke.

I didn't like his mocking tone or the horrible sneering look on his face. Actually I didn't like much about Pete at all.

'Actually it was the carriage that turned into a pumpkin, not Cinderella,' I snapped – just as the band finished a song. My words seemed to echo in the sudden silence. There were a few sniggers and several heads turned to stare. I felt my face turn crimson. What the hell was I doing, nitpicking over the technicalities of a fairytale?

Pete guffawed loudly. 'Well, I'm sure you know better than me. Off you go then, back to your fairy castle or wherever it is you princesses hang out these days.'

'Come on then,' Ellen said crossly, diving under the table to find her bag. I certainly wasn't doing much for the cool sophisticated image she was trying to portray. But right then I didn't care. All I wanted was to be out of that place.

I didn't wait for her to make her goodbyes, just rushed for the door. Outside, I moved away from the small group standing smoking and waited for Ellen, willing her to hurry up.

She appeared at my side. 'Suppose we'd better make a run for it!' she giggled, taking off her silver sandals and hitching the bag over her shoulder. We dashed down the road, Ellen squealing as she tried to avoid puddles in her bare feet. I just hoped there wasn't any shattered glass or anything else nasty lying around.

We made it back to the tennis club just in time. People were spilling out of the hall in small groups, talking and laughing. Ellen scrambled into her sandals as I looked around anxiously for Mum's car.

'Hey, where did you two get to?' demanded a voice behind me. I whirled around to see Siobhan, arm in arm with one of her cronies, eying us suspiciously.

'What's it to you …' I started to say, before Ellen interrupted me.

'What are you talking about? We had a great time, didn't we Ellen? Best disco in ages. Oh look, there's your mum!'

We hastily made our way over to Mum's car. She was scanning the crowd of teenagers, looking a little anxious. Her expression changed as she saw us approach, first relief, and then a little frown as her eyes travelled over Ellen's outfit.

'Oh no – you forgot to change back into your jeans,' I muttered, nudging her.

I tugged open the back door and we piled in. We always sit in the back together when it's just us. We've done it since we were kids, pretending to be princesses being driven around by our chauffeur.

'Hello girls. Good night?' Mum asked. She was still looking at Ellen's skirt, though she didn't say anything.

'It was brilliant, wasn't it Maggie?' Ellen said, smiling. 'Except that idiot Siobhan Brady spilled a glass of lemonade on my jeans and I had to get this skirt from the costume cupboard, can you believe it?'

As we drove away, the last thing I saw was Liam, standing at the side of the road looking after the car, a puzzled frown on his face.

Dear Ellen,

When I picture you now, you're always somewhere hot. I see you lying on a beach in a white bikini, oversized sunglasses and a giant straw hat to protect your face from the sun, paperback novel at your side where you've dropped it after falling asleep on your beach towel. Or else you're in the middle of a game of beach volleyball, leaping around the makeshift court, smashing the ball over the net and laughing with delight when your team scores. All the guys are enthralled by you, wanting to impress you, showing off. All of the girls want to be you.

Sometimes I see you walking through a city park, taking

shade from the sun under leafy green trees, swinging that same straw hat carelessly by your side. You stop to buy an ice cream from a stall, wander over to a bench to sit down and enjoy it, feed the remains of the cone to some ducks.

Sometimes you're working – I suppose you have to fund this lifestyle somehow. Usually you're a waitress, something sociable, where you can meet lots of people. You love the changing faces every day, people passing in and out of your life with their own stories, never around long enough to become stale or boring. You clear empty coffee cups from tables covered in red-checked table cloths, outside a café in a bustling square. You take your break, peeling off your apron and heading to a quiet spot by the river where you can chill out for a few minutes, watching the boats go by. Then it's back to the busy square, a bit of window-shopping – you have your eye on a pair of red shoes with killer heels, all you need is your next pay cheque and they'll be yours. Then it's back to work, greeting customers with a friendly smile and joking with the other waiting staff.

I see you in train stations, choosing your next destination by sticking a pin in a map. You throw your giant rucksack over your shoulder, not caring how much it weighs (red shoes will never weigh you down). You eat a sandwich at the noisy counter, gulping down your coffee when you realise your train's just been called. I see you making new friends, moving on, with promises to stay in touch which you know you won't keep. All those new experiences, new places, the freshness in every new day, the pace of life you've always craved.

It's never night time in these images. I don't see you crying, alone on a dark city street, scared, nowhere to stay for the night, thinking of calling home but your stubbornness getting in the way. I don't see you swigging whiskey from a bottle in a brown paper bag, pulling a sleeping bag around you, curling up in a shop front, hoping you'll be safe for the night. I don't see you held prisoner somewhere, a dark confined space, your only contact a cruel captor who brings you food and water and threats. I don't, because I don't, won't, can't let these images in, and when they try to intrude, I put my hands over my eyes and focus with all my strength on that white bikini picture, the blue of the sea, the laughter and light, and I know that's where you belong.

Love,

Maggie.

It was only when we were getting ready for bed that Ellen realised. She was looking through the texts on her phone with a puzzled look on her face.

'What the hell … oh no! This isn't my phone!' she exclaimed. 'Look!' She showed me the screen, with a list of names I didn't recognise – mostly male.

'Oh no, you must have left it in the pub,' I said. 'Did someone else have the same phone?'

'I don't know, I didn't notice. We were in such a rush I just grabbed the phone and ran!' Ellen was scrolling through the numbers on the phone. 'Maybe it belongs to someone at our table.'

'Want me to ring it?' I suggested. I really hoped she wasn't going to suggest sneaking out to go back to the pub. My nerves were already shattered.

'Good idea!'

I dialled her number. Someone answered right away. In the background I could hear the sound of talking and laughing and glasses clinking – whoever it was must still be in the pub.

'Hello? Who's this?' I asked, feeling a bit stupid.

'It's Pete. That Ellen?'

God, it would have to be Pete wouldn't it?

'No – hang on, I'll get Ellen for you,' I said hastily. I passed her the phone, hissing, 'It's that guy, Pete!'

Ellen's face lit up. 'Hello? Can you believe it, we must have got our phones mixed up! … Uh-huh. Uh-huh … yes I can meet you tomorrow. Why don't you give me a ring in the morning?'

There was a pause, then Ellen laughed. 'Nope, not too early. We princesses like our lie-ins.'

She hung up and handed me back the phone. 'We're going to meet tomorrow in town. This is excellent, I wasn't sure when I was going to see him again.'

She got into bed and snuggled down under the duvet.

'Night, Maggie. Thanks for coming tonight, it was fab!'

I lay down too, switching off the light and gazing at the stars on my ceiling. Was it possible that Ellen had taken the wrong phone on purpose?

Dear Ellen,

I thought you would like an update on Fuddy Duddy's fashion sense. I'm sorry to say it hasn't improved. Today she was wearing a snot-green dress with enormous cerise flowers all over it. Hideous. And it was too tight, which meant her enormous bust looked like it was straining to get out. I was looking at the buttons, just waiting for one of them to pop, when she realised I was staring at her and I had to quickly look away. I wish we could give her some fashion advice. It's really not fair that we should have to look at THAT every time we go to geography.

Liam has started walking home with me every day now, if he doesn't have football training after school. You'll be glad to know that we do actually talk now. Most of the time, anyway. We talk about football, or about things that have happened at school, or what we're going to do at the weekend. He tells me daft things his teachers have said, who got caught smoking behind the gym when they were supposed to be in class, and who's going out on Saturday night. I tell him what's been going on with the girls at school, who's not speaking to who, and the latest silly thing Jamie has done.

We don't ever talk about you.

Maggie.

Ellen spent the morning fretting about what to wear to meet Pete. Since she was staying in my house, her selection was somewhat more limited than usual. She changed her outfit five times and still wasn't too happy. She even thought about rushing home to get something of her own, but decided against it in the end, afraid we'd be late. I tried not to be insulted on behalf of my wardrobe.

Pete was late. We sat in Java Bay, sipping an oversized pink lemonade with two straws.

'Are you sure we'll see him from here?' Ellen asked for the third time.

'Of course. You said you'd meet him outside the Music Centre. There's only one entrance,' I reassured her.

'I'd hate him to think I stood him up,' Ellen said.

I looked at my watch. It was beginning to look like it might be the other way around.

We made the pink lemonade last as long as we could. The cafe started to fill up, and I noticed the waitress giving us some pointed looks as she cleared tables nearby.

'He's an hour late,' I said eventually. 'Do you want to text him or something?'

'No. No way. I don't want to sound desperate,' Ellen said. 'Let's go and visit Liam, see what he's up to.'

'Maybe we shouldn't. He'll be busy,' I said.

'Oh we won't keep him long,' Ellen said. 'We can just see if there's any gossip from the disco last night.'

'I thought you didn't care about that "baby disco",' I said.

'I don't.'

'So let's leave it then. We can have a look round the shoe shop instead.'

'We can do that after. I think it might be a good idea if Pete saw me talking to Liam. Make him jealous!'

She was back to scheming again, and somehow Liam and I were caught in the middle. As usual, I gave in.

Liam was carrying a huge box of books into the newsagent's. He smiled when he saw us coming. 'Well, where did you two get to last night?'

'Oh, it's a bit of a long story,' Ellen said. 'There was this band we wanted to see. Did we miss anything?'

'Not much,' Liam said, beginning to take some books out of the box and stacking them on a shelf. 'It was a good night, but nothing that exciting.'

'Obviously not, since we weren't there,' Ellen said.

'What are you up to today?' I asked, then immediately felt my face starting to go red. What sort of an idiot was I? Wasn't it obvious? 'I mean, obviously you're working now, but any plans for later? I mean, not that I'm suggesting we meet up or anything, I'm supposed to be helping my mum with something anyway ...' I trailed off. Ellen was giving me that wide-eyed look which means she is afraid to imagine what I am going to say next. I was a bit afraid myself.

Liam, lovely guy that he is, just gave me a straight answer. 'I'm working til four. Not sure after that. Should be studying but I might give myself the evening off.'

'Well, let us know what you're up to. We have to go,' Ellen said. Her – sorry, Pete's – phone had beeped and she obviously couldn't wait to check it.

'Sorry, Liam. Bye, Liam,' I babbled, turning to follow Ellen, who hadn't waited to say goodbye but was already on her way out of the shop.

'That was kind of rude,' I started.

'At least I wasn't chatting him up!' Ellen said.

'I wasn't chatting him up!'

'That's what it sounded like to me. Do you fancy him or something?'

Thankfully she didn't wait for a reply because she was reading her text at the same time. 'Damn, it's Pete, he says something's come up and he can't make it into town.'

'Nice of him to let you know!' I said, glad of the change of subject. 'We've been waiting more than an hour!'

'Oh I'm sure it must be something important or he would have come. Not to worry. At least I get more time to plan my outfit!'

'What about your phone?'

'I don't know. I suppose we can just forward any messages

to each other.' Ellen suddenly looked worried. 'God, I hope Mum doesn't send him any of her daft soppy texts!'

She put the phone back in her bag. 'How about we call over to Carrie's? I can't wait to tell her all about Pete!'

Dear Ellen,

It's school musical time again. I saw the poster up on the noticeboard. Mum wants me to audition, but what fun would it be without you?

Nothing could compare to **Grease** anyway. It was our favourite since we were little. We used to re-enact the scene in Frenchy's bedroom every time we had a sleepover, and any time one of us was telling a story about a boy the other one would start humming 'Tell me more, tell me more!' .

I don't know why they bothered holding auditions for Sandy last year. There was never any question over who would play her. You were the best singer in our year, the star of the drama classes, and the only one who still took dancing lessons. Most of us gave these up some time around the age of eight when the thrill of prancing around in a pink tutu began to wear off a bit. But you always enjoyed it. You didn't care whether it was cool or not, you did it because it was fun and you liked being watched.

Really you would have been better suited to the part of Rizzo, with her feisty attitude and rebellion against authority in any form. Timid, wishy-washy, goody-two-shoes Sandy had nothing in common with you, except that you both fancied Danny. But you were born to be a star.

Liam says he's not going to audition this year either. He says he doesn't see the point.

Love,

Maggie.

The Monday after our night out in the pub, Miss Leigh stopped me on my way to my locker. 'Maggie, I'm having a meeting tomorrow at lunchtime to talk about *Romeo and Juliet*. I hope you can come along. I'd like you to help me out with the costumes again.'

'Sure, no problem,' I said.

'Great. 1.20, OK? I'll see you then. Oh here's Ellen, the very person.' She told Ellen about the meeting and asked her to come along too. 'I can definitely picture you as a tempestuous Capulet,' she finished with a laugh.

'Did you manage to get your phone back?' I asked, when Miss Leigh had gone.

'No, he was busy all day yesterday. He said he'd text me today,' Ellen said. 'Starting to be a bit of a nuisance actually. My dad was texting me yesterday and Pete forwarded me on the texts, then I told him what to say back, then my dad texted back to say why was I using text speak when I don't normally?'

'Can't believe he noticed that!' I said.

'Oh he seems to be in a noticing sort of mood at the moment,' Ellen said. 'He must be having an attack of the guilts. Wants to take me and Robert out for dinner tomorrow.'

'Will your mum let you go?'

'I haven't asked her. I want to sort out my phone first. Dad will be sure to notice if I have the wrong one!'

The bell rang for first class.

'Eeek, I haven't got anything ready!' Ellen said, pulling books out of her bag and flinging them into her locker. 'What have we got first class?'

'English,' I said. 'Just like last Monday, and the Monday before, and the Monday before that ...'

'OK, OK, not all of us are super-organised like you!' Ellen located her novel and folder at the back of her locker. 'Here they are! OK let's get going.'

She may as well have left her stuff in her locker for all the attention she paid to Cathy and Heathcliff during that class. The elusive text from Pete came just as we were sitting down.

'Great! He wants to meet me tomorrow at lunchtime,' she whispered to me.

'But we're supposed to be going to the meeting about the play,' I whispered back.

'Oh, who cares about that?' Ellen said. 'I get enough Shakespeare in class without giving up my lunchtimes too.

You don't really want to do all that work do you?'

I said nothing. The thing was, I really did want to go to the meeting. I knew Ellen wouldn't understand, but I really enjoyed helping with the costumes. I had helped Miss Leigh with *Grease* a few months earlier. I'd got Mum to bring me round to all the charity shops at the weekends, looking for fifties clothes. She had raided the attic for me too, and so had Aunt Pat. They'd both loved *Grease* when they were teenagers and had kept all of Granny's old clothes. The two of them had been like two kids, squealing with excitement over hula hoop skirts and those blouses with the huge collars, and showing me photos of Granny and her friends and the kind of hairdos they'd had at the time.

A period drama would be even more fun. We'd have to see what we had in the acting cupboard that could be taken apart and remade into something else. We'd probably have to make a lot of things from scratch. I might even be able to do a couple of things on my sewing machine, if the school would pay for the material.

I looked over at Ellen and sighed. I could see there was no way I'd be going to the meeting. She was gazing out the window with this dreamy look on her face, still clutching the mobile with Pete's text on the screen.

Dear Ellen,

I'm sorry, I'm sorry, I'm sorry. I don't know what more I can say. We're both hurting, both missing you. That's all it is. He doesn't really like me. Not like that. He couldn't.

I know what you're thinking – what about me, what about my feelings? And yes, I have always liked him, but I never meant to act on it. He is yours – whether you want him or not.

Maggie.

I was kind of hoping Pete would text to cancel, but when I saw Ellen appear in school the next day with the pink straw bag, I knew it could only mean trouble.

'What's with the bag?' I asked, as casually as I could.

'Clothes to change into. I'm meeting Pete at lunchtime, remember?' Ellen said. Glancing over her shoulder, she opened the bag a crack to show me what was inside. Another new top. Of course.

'I know this is probably a stupid question, Ellen, but why do you have to get changed to meet him?' A thought struck me. 'He does know you're still at school, right?'

Ellen rolled her eyes at me. 'Of course he does. I had to tell him in the end. Although I may have said I was repeating my Leaving Cert.'

I sighed. The repeats don't have to wear uniform. It's their only compensation for being forced to spend another year in this place. That, and finally being treated like a grown-up by the staff. Ellen says it would almost be worth repeating. I disagree.

'What did you tell him that for? What if you bump into him some day on your way to school and he realises you lied?'

'Oh Maggie, don't start with the "what ifs" again,' Ellen said. 'I'll worry about that when the time comes. The more immediate problem is, where will I get changed?'

I considered this. 'Not here, anyway. If anyone sees you leaving in your own clothes they're bound to ask questions.'

'That's true. I'm supposed to be meeting him in the shopping centre, we'll just have to get there early and change in the toilets I think.'

'We?'

'Yes. You are coming with me, aren't you?' Ellen demanded. 'You know we're not allowed leave the school on our own. And I can't tell anyone else about this.'

I sighed. It looked like I could forget about the *Romeo and Juliet* meeting. Sneaking around corners with Ellen and minding her uniform while she met Pete was obviously so much more important.

I felt guilty walking out the school gate. So ridiculous. We hadn't even done anything wrong. Ellen was flitting between being absolutely hyper and clamming up with nerves. It was kind of exhausting actually.

We squeezed into a cubicle in the ladies' toilets, and Ellen started to wriggle out of her clothes.

'Oh, I've just thought,' she said, pausing with her shirt half over her head. 'What are we going to do about you? You haven't got any ordinary clothes.'

'Don't worry. I'm pretty sure it's not me Pete's coming to see.'

'But I don't want him to think I'm some kind of saddo, hanging out with one of the juniors,' Ellen said.

'Oh, thanks a lot!' I pretended to be offended, but couldn't help laughing. 'Don't worry. I wasn't planning on coming with you. I'll just mind your uniform and go for a look around the shops.'

'Oh Maggie, you're a star. What would I do without you?'

'Let's just hope we never have to find out!'

I lurked outside the newsagents, wanting to make sure Pete turned up this time. I flicked through a magazine, using it as cover. Ellen was sipping a sparkling water and admiring her purple nail varnish.

Pete showed up, only five minutes late, much to my surprise. He leaned in and gave Ellen a peck on the cheek. She turned scarlet.

'Hi Maggie. Ellen not with you today?'

I turned around, flustered. It was Mrs Kennedy, Liam's mum, armed with bags of coins, which she proceeded to empty into the till.

'Oh, erm, no, she's just doing something else,' I said, shoving the magazine back on the shelf.

'What have you got there?' asked Mrs Kennedy, indicating the pink straw bag. Ellen's school jumper was poking out the top.

'Oh, nothing special. Just my school jumper. I'm getting it mended.' Now it was my turn to go red.

'Let me have a look at it for you,' Mrs Kennedy said, coming out from behind the till. 'I'm a dab hand with a needle and thread.'

I took a step backwards, banging into a display of Mills and Boon books. 'There's no need, really. Thanks all the same. Oh look, you have a customer. I'd better let you go.' I backed out of the shop, feeling very grateful to the elderly man who was approaching the counter with his newspaper.

'It's no trouble. Pop back in any time,' Mrs Kennedy called, as I rushed out the door, pushing Ellen's jumper firmly back inside the bag.

I looked quickly at the cafe as I hurried past, but I couldn't see Ellen or Pete.

The next half hour passed slowly. I bought a cheese sandwich in a plastic packet from the supermarket. The cheese was overprocessed and rubbery. I munched on it as I walked around the shopping centre, but I ended up throwing most of it in the bin. I had a look in the music shop, but soon got tired of that. I'd already looked through everything on Saturday. Celine's were having a sale so I tried on a couple of things, but even with 20 per cent off I knew I didn't have enough money.

Miss Leigh had probably finished handing out extracts from the script and planning the auditions by now. She'd have moved on to set design and costumes. She was probably wondering where I was. Maybe she would ask Carrie to help her instead.

Ellen's bag was starting to feel heavy. I sat down on the bench near the toilets, where I'd arranged to meet her at ten to two, so she could change back into her uniform. I was five minutes early, but I'd had enough of walking around. I took out *Wuthering Heights* and started checking over the section we were supposed to read for that afternoon.

I ended up getting absorbed in Heathcliff's rantings, and when I looked up at the clock again it was five to two. Where was Ellen? I scanned the corridor in both directions, but couldn't see her distinctive mop of red hair anywhere. I wondered if she might have walked past my bench and gone straight into the Ladies, so I looked in there too. No sign of her.

Three minutes to two. Ellen was really cutting it fine. She still needed to change her clothes, and it would take us at least five minutes to get back to school. We had maths first thing, and old Bouncer had been pretty huffy with Ellen since the April Fools joke.

I decided to walk casually past the cafe. I didn't want to

embarrass Ellen by actually going up to her, but hopefully she would just see me and realise the time.

She wasn't sitting at the table outside, where she had been earlier, but then she hadn't been there when I walked past the second time either. Maybe they had moved to a table inside. Pete looked like a guy who didn't enjoy too much exposure to natural daylight.

I hesitated. Should I go in or not? I could always just go up to the counter and buy a bottle of water. But then Pete might see me too.

Just then Mrs Kennedy came out of the newsagents. Decision made – I darted into the cafe before she could see me and start talking about the jumper again, or comment on the fact that I should be back in school by now.

They definitely weren't in the cafe. I wandered back to the door, checking to make sure Mrs Kennedy was nowhere in sight. Not knowing what else to do, I headed back towards the toilets, even though something told me she wasn't going to be there. I sat back down on my bench and looked up at the clock. Five past two.

What now? This was getting a bit ridiculous – what was Ellen doing that was so important she could just leave me hanging around waiting for her and making us late for school?

I checked my phone, just in case she had rung, but of course she hadn't. I thought about ringing her, but I didn't know which phone to ring. She and Pete might have swapped back right away, or they might have been too busy familiarising themselves with each other's tonsils. The last thing I wanted was to have to speak to Pete. I decided to send a text to her own phone and just hope she'd get it.

The shopping centre was starting to empty, as people went back to school and work. I felt really self-conscious sitting there in my uniform, Ellen's pink bag at my feet. I felt like all the sales assistants would know that I should be back at school by now. At least I couldn't be seen from the newsagents – that was some comfort.

I wondered if I should go back to school on my own, but then I dismissed that idea right away. If Ellen came back to school with no uniform, she'd be in even bigger trouble than just for being late. And both of us would be in trouble for being out on our own.

Feeling really annoyed now, I checked my phone again, but it was still blank. I would kill her when I saw her, I really would.

Just then I spotted Mrs Kennedy coming in my direction. Without really thinking I grabbed Ellen's bag and bolted in the opposite direction. I circled round the shopping centre, made sure she was nowhere in sight and then dashed out the main entrance.

OK, there was clearly no point in hanging around the shopping centre. Ellen had my number, she could text me when she finally came to her senses. Just in case, I sent a text to both mobiles, saying that I was going to start walking back towards the school.

As I walked up the main street I felt like all eyes were on me again. I told myself not to be stupid. There could be any number of reasons I could legitimately be out of school at this time. I could be on my way back from the dentist, or the doctor. I could have a free class, and be doing an errand for a teacher.

I went the long way around though, away from the primary school. Mum would be picking up Jamie shortly, and she'd certainly see straight through any story.

My phone rang. I dropped the pink bag in my scramble to answer it on time, and Ellen's uniform started to spill out onto the path.

'Ellen, where are you?' I demanded, holding the phone between my ear and shoulder as I tried to stuff the clothes back into the bag.

'Keogh's,' Ellen said.

The pub where we'd seen Flaming Moes.

'What the hell are you doing there?'

I could hear Pete saying something to her in the background, and she giggled and shushed him. 'Pete said their toasted sandwiches are the best in town. Look Maggie, I'm really sorry I'm late, I just lost track of time. Can you meet me here instead? We're just inside the door.'

'Ellen. I am in my *school uniform*,' I said.

'Oh, right. Erm, well will you meet me out the back? Oh wait, I know. Go to the laneway beside the pub. The window to the ladies looks out on that. You can pass me in my clothes, and I'll get changed as quick as I can.'

'You are going to get us both suspended,' I said. 'I'm so tempted to go right back up to the school.' I had already started walking in the direction of Keogh's, but there was no need for Ellen to know that just yet.

'Oh come on, Maggie. Think of it as an adventure,' Ellen said. 'Next time I'll bring clothes for you too, OK?'

'Next time I'll go to the meeting like I wanted to and you can go on your own.'

'Maggie, please ...'

'I'll see you in five minutes,' I sighed.

The laneway to the side of Keogh's was filthy, filled with empty crates. I stepped gingerly through the broken glass. I tried to breathe through my nose and to not think about where the smell was coming from.

'Ellen,' I hissed when I got to the window. 'Are you there?'

Ellen's face appeared at the window. 'Maggie, you're a life-saver. Throw in the bag, quick.'

I stood on a beer crate to reach up to the small open window and passed her the bag. 'Is Pete still there?'

'Yes but he's with his mates. I think I'll just slip away and send him a text later.'

I waited while Ellen changed.

'Maggie, can you bring over some more of those beer crates? I'm going to climb out the window.'

'Are you crazy? You'll break your neck.'

'I'll be fine. It's not that far down. What else can I do? I can't go back into the pub in my school uniform, and there's nowhere else for me to get changed.'

I sighed. Sometimes Ellen's logic was like no one else's, but on this occasion there really didn't seem to be another option.

I brought over a second beer crate and stacked it on top of the first one. Ellen balanced precariously on the wash-hand basin for a moment before scrambling out the window. Her jumper caught on the hinge and tore. I couldn't help smiling at the irony, even as I helped her climb down.

Ellen didn't care – she was too busy shoving all her clothes into the pink bag. Her face was looking suspiciously red.

'Ellen were you drinking?' I demanded.

'Just a couple of vodkas. Should make maths a bit more bearable don't you think?'

'You're even more crazy than I thought! Come on, let's get going.'

We hurried up the hill towards the school. There was only fifteen minutes left of maths. Bouncer was going to hit the roof.

Ellen's phone beeped. 'That'll be Pete, wondering where

I've disappeared to,' she said. 'He'll probably think I've turned into a pumpkin again!' She got a fit of the giggles as we sneaked in the side entrance to the school.

'Shush, you eejit – we're trying not to be seen!' I hissed at her.

'Sorry – just thinking of Pete sitting there wondering where I've got to,' she said.

Luckily Bouncer's classroom was at the back of the school so we didn't need to go near the secretary's office. If she'd seen us coming in we'd have been made to sign the late book.

'What are we going to say?' I asked Ellen. I'd been racking my brains for a good excuse but hadn't come up with anything.

'Leave it to me,' Ellen said.

We opened the door to Bouncer's room. He was standing at the board writing out an equation. He turned to look at us with an expression that was more shocked than angry. 'Nice of you to turn up, ladies.'

'Sorry, sir,' I said meekly. 'We, erm ...'

'I had an emergency,' Ellen said. 'Women's problems. Maggie helped me out.'

I felt myself blushing, but it was nothing compared to Bouncer – his face was now the colour of the poppies on his tie. 'All right. Sit down and get out your books.'

Ellen flashed me a look of pure triumph. She'd used the

one excuse a male teacher would never dream of questioning.

I sank into my seat and sent up a silent prayer for a few hours free of drama.

Dear Ellen,

Actually though, why should I be sorry? Liam isn't your boyfriend. He would have been if you'd let him, but you never even fancied him. You had plenty of chances if you'd wanted to be with him. But there was always someone more exciting for you than the boy next door. And anyway, he was the one who kissed me.

So why do I feel like I've betrayed you?

Still your friend,

Maggie.

Over the next few weeks I hardly got to spend any time with Ellen on our own. At school, there was always someone around. Even walking from one classroom to another we would be surrounded by girls. Word had got out that Ellen was going out with a guy who was involved with A Band. It didn't matter that the band in question played in grubby little pubs for beer money, or that Pete wasn't even a proper band member, just someone who helped set up their equipment, and occasionally played bass guitar when the normal guy was too drunk.

Ellen was maintaining the charade with Pete that she was

repeating her Leaving Cert, so he didn't wait for her outside the school gates, as other people's boyfriends did, and if she met him at lunchtime she always used me for cover. After she'd made me late that first time I didn't want to do it again, but she said she was sorry about a million times and pestered me so much I gave in. Anyway, I realised it was going to be the only way I would get to see her, and snatched minutes with Ellen were better than nothing at all.

She didn't involve anyone else in these sneaky little excursions from school, so hardly anyone had seen Pete, which only added to his mystique. Carrie had seen them going into a pub together one evening, and reported back that he was tall and skinny and dark, and faintly dangerous looking.

When she wasn't off drinking with Pete, or changing her clothes in cramped toilet cubicles, she seemed to be spending a lot of time looking after Robert. Some days I'd see him outside our school after the primary school day ended, waiting for Ellen to be finished. It looked as though Mrs B had forgotten to collect him again. I thought about suggesting to Ellen that I get Mum to collect him along with Jamie, but I didn't want to embarrass her. If Robert was waiting, Ellen would dash out the door to meet him as soon as the last bell went, not even waiting to go to her locker. This meant she was forever turning up at school without her homework done, or (less often) ringing me and getting me to read sections out to her over the phone, and doing her homework that way.

If Robert wasn't waiting, I might get to chat to Ellen at her locker for a few minutes, and she would gleefully tell me the latest on Pete and the band, and try to talk me into going along to the next gig. But some days I had a meeting with Miss Leigh and Carrie. The three of us were working on the costumes for *Romeo and Juliet*. Miss Leigh had forgiven me for missing the first three meetings (all due to Ellen-related crises), or possibly she had decided that, unreliable though I might be, the school had a limited number of students who were willing to spend their spare time sewing.

Ellen had point-blank refused all Miss Leigh's entreaties to take part in the play. To Miss Leigh she said she was too busy studying and couldn't spare the time. To me she said she couldn't bear *Romeo and Juliet* because there was so much weeping and wailing and soul-searching and then they all just died in the end. I think the truth was that she had so much going on in her life that she had no room to cram something else in which she wouldn't be able to properly commit to. Ellen never did things by halves. She either threw herself in body and soul, or else she didn't bother at all.

I was strangely glad to have something that was nothing to do with Ellen. It was probably the first time in our lives that I'd found something that I was good at, just on my own, and not being Ellen's supporting act.

Dear Ellen,

How could you leave Robert? That's the bit I really don't understand. You adore that kid. At least you used to. I know you used to join in my moans about how annoying little brothers are, but you would have done anything for him. You did do everything for him, for a long time, when your mother wasn't able to cope. All those times you brought him to football, washed his gear afterwards, made his packed lunch for school, checked his homework. Don't you ever wonder who's doing all that for him now?

Even before your parents separated, you were always the devoted big sister. Maybe no one else would have noticed – you detested soppiness of any kind, so you certainly did a good job of hiding it. But I knew. Remember the time some boys at school were teasing Robert about still having stabilisers on his bike? You spent hours one Saturday afternoon teaching him to ride his bike without stabilisers. And then you went into school with him on Monday and told the biggest of the bullies that if he teased Robert again you'd punch him in the nose.

And then you just leave him behind. You take off for your new life, wherever you are, and you leave Robert to deal with everything on his own, being piggy in the middle in your parents' fights, taunts from bullies, problems with his homework. You just leave him, and don't even check in to see how he's doing. How could you?

Maggie.

The sewing club, as we'd started to call ourselves, met after school on a Thursday. I was working on a nightdress for Juliet. Miss Leigh had given me some old curtains, and I was using the material from them. They were a soft ivory coloured lace. The edges were a bit yellow from age, but Miss Leigh thought they would come out all right in the wash, and if they didn't it didn't really matter. As I sewed, I pictured Juliet standing on her balcony, her ivory robes flowing down to her feet, and Romeo standing underneath declaring his love for her. I wondered if anyone would ever love me that much.

Mum collected me after our hour was up. 'How did it go today?' she asked.

'Fine. Juliet's nightie is nearly done,' I said.

'Ellen's not in your sewing club, is she?'

'Oh Mum, can you really picture Ellen sitting around sewing costumes for someone else? She's not even going to be in the play.'

Mum started the car. 'I was just wondering, because Robert left his football kit in the car this afternoon.'

'Oh, did you give him a lift?'

'Yes. He was standing outside the school on his own. It seemed like Paula had forgotten to collect him. Is everything OK with them do you know?'

'What do you mean?'

'Just that I kind of get the impression she isn't coping too well with the separation.'

I said nothing.

Mum pressed on. 'Has Ellen said anything?'

'Like what?'

'Like, you know. That her mum is struggling a bit. That things aren't too happy at home.'

'Not really. You know what Ellen's like. She never really talks about anything too deep.'

'Maybe I'll call in and see how Paula is. I'm sure she'll be wondering about Robert's kit, too.'

I was sure she wouldn't even have noticed, but I didn't say so. I didn't think Ellen would want me talking about them like this. She probably wouldn't be too happy about Mum barging in like some kind of social worker trying to solve all their problems, either.

We parked outside Ellen's house. When we got out of the car, we could hear the screaming right away. My heart sank. There were two voices, Ellen's high-pitched and indignant, Mrs B's screechy and almost out of control.

'It's only a bit of vodka! It's not like I'm doing drugs or something.'

'You're underage. It's illegal!'

'Oh big deal! Everyone our age gets drunk every now and then!'

Mum raised her eyebrows at me. I shrugged and tried to look innocent.

'That doesn't make it acceptable young lady! And as for drinking alone in your bedroom ...'

'Oh you're one to talk!'

'What's that supposed to mean?'

'I've seen the stash of bottles you've hidden under the stairs! Some example you are! You're just a pathetic old drunk!'

I heard a loud crack and Ellen screamed. I was about to rush to the door, but Mum put her hand on my arm to stop me. 'Don't, Maggie. We'll only make things worse if we go in now.' She hesitated a moment, then left Robert's bag on the doorstep. 'I'll try to come back and talk to Paula tomorrow.'

Dear Ellen,

I saw your mum today. She was wandering down Main Street, just staring into shop windows, as if she'd forgotten what she came out for and was hoping something would jog her memory. She had no coat on, even though it was quite a cold day, and her top didn't match her skirt, and had an orange stain down the front. She looked so lost and alone I wanted to go over to her, but I didn't know what to say.

I kept thinking of how there were once four of you, until people started dropping off. Like ten green bottles. First your dad. Then you. And now my mum says your dad is trying to get custody of Robert. He wants your mum to be declared an unfit mother, just because she's not coping very well.

School was horrible today too. I came up behind Orla and Stephanie when they were talking at their lockers, and I heard them saying something about Carrie's party. Then when they realised I was there they got all embarrassed and changed the subject. I didn't say anything, just started sorting out my books and ignored them.

I wonder why Carrie didn't invite me?

Love,

Maggie.

She didn't, though. Mum, I mean. She didn't go back the next day to talk to Mrs B, and when she did see her again, it was too late. I think Mum blames herself for that more than anything.

In school, Ellen said nothing about what had happened. I had texted her to say where we'd left Robert's gear, and she'd sent me a one-word reply – 'Thanks' – so I think she knew we'd overheard her. But the only reference she made to it was when I caught her sneaking a bottle of vodka into her locker.

'Ellen, you lunatic! If you get caught with that you'll be expelled!'

Ellen tossed her head. She always did have an impressive range of head tosses, from contemptuous to flirtatious. This one was most definitely of the dismissive kind. 'I won't leave it there. Not going to risk a random locker search. But

Mum's on the warpath so I can't leave it at home. I just need to think of somewhere.'

'In the toilets?' I suggested.

'Where, though? There aren't any cupboards or anything like that.'

'Emmm ... how about in a toilet cistern?'

Ellen made a face. 'Ew, yuck. Actually though, it's a good idea ... thanks Maggie. Shhh, here comes Carrie.' She slammed her locker shut and turned to greet Carrie with her dazzling smile. 'Hi, Carrie. What's up?'

'Just wanted to let you know I'm having a party to celebrate the end of the exams.'

'Oh brilliant, when's it on?' asked Ellen.

'Saturday week. My parents are going to be away for the night, so I've got a free house.'

'Great,' I said. 'Count me in.'

'Me too!' said Ellen. 'Sounds great.'

I was so glad Ellen was enthusiastic about it; it seemed like the kind of thing the new Ellen would have scoffed at as beneath her.

'Maybe you can bring your new mystery man?' Carrie suggested, with a knowing smile. 'All the girls are dying to meet him.'

'We'll see. He may have a gig or something. Saturday nights are a busy time for him you know.'

'Well, do your best! And get him to bring the rest of the

band.'

Ellen's mobile rang, and she moved away to answer it. Carrie turned to me. 'I can't wait for this party. It's just been so crazy lately with getting the costumes finished for the play and then having to start studying for the exams.'

'I know, it's been mental,' I said. 'It'll be great to have the party to look forward to afterwards. Will your parents really let you have people over when they're away?'

'They said it was fine as long as Jane was there,' Carrie said. 'Just because she's the oldest, Mum seems to think she's super responsible. She's having her friends over the next night, I said I wanted the first night just for mine. You know what some of her boring friends are like!'

The bell rang, and we moved off towards our first class.

'You're friends with Liam Kennedy, aren't you?' Carrie said.

'Oh ... em ... sort of,' I said.

'Invite him, will you? And tell him to bring his mates. We need some more boys.' Carrie glanced back at Ellen, who was still on the phone. 'I'd ask Ellen to say it to him, but she's a bit weird about him, isn't she?'

'What do you mean?' I asked.

'Like there's some kind of history there.'

'No. They're just friends,' I said. I knew it wasn't the whole story, but I also knew I couldn't begin to explain it to Carrie when I didn't even understand it myself.

'Well, good. Let me know what he says, OK? And invite whoever else you want – just not too many girls!'

Dear Ellen,

Do you remember the time Carrie threw her first big sleepover party? We desperately wanted to go, but we didn't think we'd be allowed. We were only eight, and the only time we'd slept over at someone's house was at each other's. So you had the bright idea that you would tell your mum that I was allowed to go, and I'd tell my mum that you were allowed.

When I brought it up with Mum I was hoping she'd just agree right away, but expecting that she'd probably come out with her usual, 'And if Ellen stuck her hand in the fire would you stick your hand in the fire?'. She didn't though. She just gave me a suspicious look, and went off to phone your mum. So much for our great plan!

But they must have understood how badly we wanted to go. Or maybe they just thought we'd be fine since we had each other. Either way, they gave in and we got to go to the party.

Do you remember how excited we were? I got new pyjamas especially, and you got a new backpack. There were eight of us – eight eight-year-olds, we thought we were so cool and grown up. We stayed up later than I'd ever been up before, even for Aunt Pat's New Year's Eve parties. Orla was terrified by the ghost stories, and said she wanted to go home, but we talked her out of it by offering her the last of the chocolate swirl ice cream. Carrie even said she could sleep in her bed, instead of in a sleeping bag on the floor.

Carrie's parents eventually got fed up of all our messing around. I think it was Orla and Carrie bouncing on the bed and knocking a picture off the wall that was the last straw. They came in and told us in no uncertain terms that if we didn't go to sleep at once they would phone our parents and ask them to come and collect us.

Poor Carrie was mortified. She had been trying so hard to make her party the kind that would be talked about for months. In a good way, I mean. And it still was, of course. Carrie's parties have been legendary ever since.

This is the first one I wasn't invited to. It only struck me afterwards that she's been avoiding me in school too. All that crowd have.

I don't blame Orla for getting spooked by the ghost stories. I still get a shiver down my spine when I think of the one about the woman in the car, and the maniac in the back seat, waiting for his chance to kill her.

Love,

Maggie.

One week before the party, it was Ellen's dad's weekend to have her.

'You've got to come too,' Ellen begged me.

I didn't think this was a good idea. 'He only gets you one

weekend a month. I'm sure he wants to spend time with just you and Robert.'

'But Robert can't go!' Ellen said. 'He's going away camping with the Scouts. He's going to Dad's next weekend instead.'

'Well, why can't you go next weekend too?' I asked.

'Duhhhh,' Ellen said, whacking her hand on her forehead. 'Because Carrie's party is on! Dad won't want me to go. He'll say it's his only chance to spend some time with me blah blah blah blah blah.'

I sighed. 'OK. I'll go if you really want me to. And if Mum says I can.' I have to admit, part of me was hoping Mum would just say no.

'Oh thank you, thank you, thank you,' Ellen grabbed my hands and whirled me around. 'You've saved me from an excruciating game of piggy in the middle with Dad and the Homewrecker. Plus Dad really likes you. He thinks you're a good influence.'

A good influence. Well, it makes a change from Sensible, or So Reliable, or Such a Good Girl. All the things I wish I wasn't, but don't know where to start not being.

Mum said yes, of course. Ellen asked her for me, when she picked us up from school, so I had no chance of getting out of it.

Ellen's dad collected us from Java Bay. 'So, what do you two ladies fancy doing this afternoon?'

Ellen said she wanted to go shopping, because she absolutely needed a new jacket for school, and some sparkly shoes to go with her sparkly top, and some boring things like a new folder and some pencils for art. Her dad laughed and said that he thought that could be arranged.

'And then can we go to the cinema, to the early showing, and then to Pizza Hut for dinner?'

I grinned to myself. Ellen obviously didn't want to go to the later show in the cinema in case anyone would see her with her dad, as if she was a child.

'Cinema sounds good.' Her dad kept his eyes firmly on the road, even though we had just stopped at a red light, and weren't going to be moving any time soon. 'About tonight though. I'm really sorry, sweetheart, but I have a work thing I have to go to. I can order a takeaway pizza for you girls though, and we can pick up a couple of DVDs. You can have a girls' night in, then I'll take you out for pancakes in the morning, OK?'

'You're going out?' Ellen said in disbelief. 'On the one night I'm staying over?'

'Sorry, sweetheart. I can't help it. It just came up.'

'I suppose the Homewrecker is going too,' Ellen snapped.

Mr B looked annoyed. 'I've asked you not to use that word, Ellen. Yes, Sandra will be there, but that's got nothing to do with it. Some very important clients are in town, and I have to take them out for dinner.'

'On the ONE night I'm here,' Ellen repeated.

'If I could change it I would,' her dad said. 'Why don't you come over next Saturday with Robert? We'll do something nice, just the three of us.'

'Forget it,' Ellen said. 'I'm busy next Saturday. If you can't change your plans for me, I'm certainly not going to change mine for you.'

I pretended to be deeply engrossed in my mobile, reading the same text again and again. Why did Ellen always have to row with her parents in front of me? It was so embarrassing. Though I definitely didn't blame her for being mad.

Ellen barely spoke to her father for the rest of the day. I tried to cover up the silences a bit by answering all his questions and chatting about Jamie and Robert. I even ended up choosing the DVD, because Ellen wouldn't. I chose *Mamma Mia*, thinking it might cheer Ellen up. She loves musicals.

Mr B's new house was like something out of a film. The entrance hall was huge, with an oak staircase, and acres of snow white carpet. The kitchen was tiled in black and white and filled with shiny gadgets and appliances, although the coffee maker was the only thing that looked like it had actually been used. I couldn't imagine Robert's muddy football boots trekking across the carpet, or his artwork stuck to the stainless steel American fridge freezer, which didn't have so much as a smudged fingerprint on it.

Ellen brightened up a lot as soon as Mr B left for his work thing (after about twenty more apologies).

'So what kind of pizza do you want?' she asked.

'Veggie, I guess. At least that way we're getting some of our five a day.'

She rolled her eyes at me. 'I don't think a few peppers is going to turn pizza into a health food, but OK.'

She picked up the phone and dialled the local pizza place. 'Hi, can I get some food delivered please? A large veggie pizza – no gross mushrooms though. Two diet Cokes. Some wedges. Oh and two tubs of Häagen Dazs please.'

'Ellen,' I hissed, 'I'm not sure we've got enough money.'

For answer, Ellen simply held up her dad's credit card and smiled. She read out the details over the phone. 'How long will that be? Great, thanks.'

She hung up the phone. 'He said about half an hour. How about doing a bit of internet shopping while we wait? Darling Daddy's treat.'

'Oh Ellen, I don't think we should,' I began.

'Oh Maggie, don't start going all goody-two-shoes on me,' Ellen said. She leaned against the kitchen counter and switched on her dad's laptop. 'If he's not going to spend time with his only daughter, the least he can do is get me a few treats. Anything you'd like? How about some new fashion books? Or do you need some material?'

'I'm going to watch the DVD. You're welcome to come and join me when you've finished spending money that's not yours.'

I marched into the sitting room, hoping Ellen would decide internet fraud wasn't as much fun without an audience. She followed me into the sitting room, sighing. I took no notice and put on the DVD. Within a few minutes she'd forgotten she was annoyed with me and was singing along with the soundtrack.

I'm not sure if it was the enormous meal of pizza, wedges and ice cream, or just the film, but I dozed off on the couch. When I woke, Ellen was in the kitchen, talking to someone on the phone.

'That was Pete,' she announced. 'He's going to come over. You don't mind, do you?'

'No,' I said automatically, but I did mind. This was supposed to be a girls' night in, not Pete and Ellen snogging on the couch while Maggie plays gooseberry.

Ellen must have known what I was thinking. 'Don't worry, he's bringing a few of his mates too. One of them is the drummer from the band. He's really cute.'

'Cute, as in actually cute, or cute, as in, he's a complete minger but he'll keep me occupied so you can have some alone time with Pete?'

'Oh Maggie, you're so cynical. He's cute cute. Not as cute as Pete maybe, but then who is?'

It was a pretty grim outlook, if Pete was the new standard against which all males would be judged.

'Won't your dad mind?' I asked. I could just imagine what

my dad would have to say if he arrived home to find a gang of older guys he didn't know lounging around in his sitting room.

'He won't be home on time,' Ellen said. 'Those work things always run really late. I'll make sure Pete and his mates are long gone by the time he gets home.'

Ellen started to tidy up the empty pizza boxes. I took the ice cream bowls into the kitchen and put them in the dishwasher. When I got back into the sitting room Ellen was standing precariously on the edge on an armchair, examining her dad's CD collection. 'God, Dad has the worst taste in music,' she complained. 'I can't put on any of this stuff. Who the hell is Prince?'

'No idea. He must have something that will do? Beatles, Elvis?'

'Nope, they're way too cool for my dad. What are we going to do? These guys are in a band. They'll think I don't know anything about music.'

'What about your iPod?' I suggested. 'Doesn't your dad have a docking station?'

Ellen's face brightened immediately. 'I'd forgotten about that. It's in his bedroom I think. I'll go and get it. You see if there's any beer in the fridge.'

'Ellen, we can't just give them your dad's beer!' I objected. 'He'd definitely notice that!'

'Well, see how many there are,' Ellen said over her shoulder as she left the room. 'I'm sure he hasn't counted them!'

I checked the fridge. There were eight bottles of beer, which was kind of an unfortunate number – big enough that Ellen would think it was OK to hand them round to the band, but small enough that Mr B couldn't possibly not notice that some were missing.

Ellen reappeared with the docking station, plugged it in beside the TV and started flicking through the playlists.

The doorbell rang, and Ellen rushed to open it. Pete stood on the doorstep. He was wearing a long-sleeved black T-shirt with a heavy metal band on the front, and there were stains on his jeans. His hair hung loose around his face, greasy and lank. Beside him stood a smaller guy, similarly dressed, though at least his jeans were clean. I recognised him as the drummer from the band. Cute he was not.

I peered over his shoulder, but there was no one else there. I wasn't exactly dying to see the rest of the band, but just two of them was even worse, especially when one of them was going out with one of us.

'You found us! Come on in,' Ellen said, grabbing Pete's arm. 'Hi, Spider. This is my friend Maggie.'

'The one I was telling you about,' Pete said, nudging him.

'Hey,' said Spider, raising one hand in a kind of half-wave. He followed Pete into the hall.

Ellen was talking at top speed, as she often does when she's nervous. 'Come on through. I've got some music on. Do you like Electrified? I love this new album. It's kind of like Flaming Moes, don't you think? What can I get you to drink?'

By this time we were all seated in the sitting room, Ellen with the two guys on the couch, Pete in the middle. I'd settled myself in an armchair as far from Spider as possible without being too obvious.

Ellen jumped up again just as soon as she had sat down and stood like a waitress waiting to take their orders.

'What kind of beer do you have?' Pete asked.

'Only Becks I'm afraid. I'd have got some more in if I'd known you were coming, but it was kind of a spur of the moment thing,' Ellen said.

Or they could have brought something with them, I thought, instead of turning up on the doorstep with one arm as long as the other, as my mum would say. They knew we were still at school and had no money, whereas presumably they had some kind of an income, even if it was only the dole.

'Becks will do fine,' Pete said. He spread his arms out along the back of the couch and surveyed the room, taking in the huge plasma TV and the solitary photo of Ellen and Robert on the mantelpiece.

Ellen was gone a long time getting the drinks. I wished I'd offered to go instead. The silence stretched on. Feeling desperately uncomfortable, I searched for something to talk about. Although Pete and Spider (what a ridiculous name) seemed happy enough just sitting. Spider was drumming his fingers on his knees in time with the beat from Ellen's iPod.

Eventually I said, 'Any gigs coming up?'

'We're playing Keogh's again next Saturday,' said Spider.

'Oh … that's nice,' I said. He didn't respond, and I couldn't think of a single other thing to say to them. We had nothing in common except Ellen.

Ellen came back in with four bottles of beer. 'Sorry I was so long. I went to the garage to get more beer to stick in the fridge.'

She passed around the beers and the three of them started talking about bands, and some obscure singer who's written a novel which is due out later this year, and how to get your hands on a draft copy on the net. I took tiny sips from my beer and wondered what exactly Pete had told Spider about me.

I soon found out. I was in the kitchen, emptying a large bag of nachos into a bowl, when Spider came in.

'So, you're the fairy tale princess then, are you?' he asked. 'How does that work then? Do you have to disappear on the stroke of midnight?'

I didn't much like the way he was looking at me. As if I was something he thought he might quite like to eat or something.

'Not exactly,' I said, trying to laugh it off. 'It's just my folks are pretty strict about curfew – you know how parents can be.'

He smiled. 'No parents to worry about tonight, though. You're staying over, right?'

What exactly was he planning? 'Well, yes, but Ellen's dad will be back later.'

'Not too soon, I hope.'

Suddenly he was standing behind me and had his arm around my waist. I felt panic rise up within my throat. I moved away, reaching into a cupboard for some dips, taking a deep breath and deciding to act like nothing had happened. 'Do you like chilli, or sour cream and onion? Or both, should I just put out both?'

'What I'd really like,' he murmured, coming over and standing far too close to me again, though not touching this time, 'is to find out what princesses taste like.'

He ran his tongue along his lip in what he seemed to think was a flirtatious gesture, but which just made me want to vomit.

'Ha, ha, none of that on the menu tonight I'm afraid.' I tried to keep my voice light and breezy. I stepped away again, holding the bowl of nachos between us. Once more he moved after me. I had to fight every instinct not to just drop the bowl and run.

'Let's go back in to the others, will we? I'm sure they're wondering where we've got to.'

'I'm sure they've got better things to worry about,' Spider

said. 'You don't want to disturb the love birds, now do you?'

Somehow I'd crossed the room and was at the sitting room door. I glanced over my shoulder, not wanting to turn my back on him. Ellen and Pete were on the couch practically welded together from the lips down. Well, too bad, I thought. Ellen had asked me to spend the weekend with her, not to hide out in the kitchen fighting off Spider just to keep him away from her and Pete.

'Anyone for nachos?' I said loudly, pushing the door open with my hip. It swung shut behind me, right in Spider's face. I pretended not to notice.

I tried not to look at Ellen and Pete as they reluctantly moved apart, concentrating instead on lowering the bowl of nachos onto the coffee table without toppling the tower of dips in my other hand.

'Nachos. Great,' Ellen said, leaning forward and grabbing a handful.

Spider had come silently into the room and sat down in the armchair I'd been in. I wondered briefly about his nickname. Had he got it from the way he crept quietly in and out of rooms, like some horrible creepy-crawly? Or was it because of those long, skinny limbs? Either way, I decided, it suited him.

Pete was nuzzling on Ellen's neck again. She squealed and half-heartedly pushed him away.

I needed to keep them talking. I couldn't be left alone

with Spider, and his horrible creepy crawly hands.

'When did you say the gig was in Keogh's?'

'Next Saturday,' Pete said, with exaggerated slowness. 'We could write it down for you.'

I pretended not to notice his tone. 'Oh that's too bad, we're going to a party that night, aren't we Ellen?'

'Yeah, just some girl in school,' Ellen said dismissively.

'Didn't think gigs were really your scene, anyway,' Pete said to me. 'No ballgowns, or handsome princes, or glass slippers. That's more your kind of thing, isn't it?'

Ellen laughed. 'Actually Maggie's more into sitting at home sewing while other people go to the ball.' She avoided my eyes.

I couldn't believe what she was saying. I felt sick to my stomach, and I pressed my hands down on my knees to try to stop them shaking. Did Ellen really care so much about impressing Pete that she could be so downright nasty?

'Oh, I don't know, I think Maggie would enjoy it just fine,' Spider said, grinning. 'Come to our next gig. We'll even make sure you get a backstage pass.'

Pete was whispering something in Ellen's ear. She suddenly jumped up, still holding his hand. 'Pete and I are going to get some more beer. Back in a minute.' She led him into the kitchen.

Spider barely waited for the door to swing closed behind them before moving over to sit on the edge of my armchair.

He stretched his arm out behind my back. 'So, what is it that does get you going then?'

'Not you, anyway,' I snapped. I moved away from him and grabbed a handful of nachos, just for something to do. I stuffed one in my mouth and tried to chew, but my mouth felt dry and there was a lump in my throat that I couldn't swallow.

'Oh come on, I'm not so bad once you get to know me. Why don't you give me a chance? Ellen says you're not seeing anyone right now. Actually I think she said you'd never had a proper boyfriend.'

He put his arm around me again and slipped a hand under my top. I stiffened, panic-stricken, not knowing what to do. The light went off in the kitchen, and I felt a momentary relief, expecting to see Ellen and Pete reappear. But then I heard footsteps on the stairs, and a muffled giggle. She was taking him upstairs and leaving me alone with this creep! I couldn't believe Ellen would abandon me like this. We had always been there for each other – even as a little five-year-old in Junior Infants she had stood up for me. Now she was just leaving me with this horrible guy I didn't even know. The feeling of betrayal was overwhelming.

Just then Spider slipped a finger inside my bra and leaned in towards me, his breath smelling of beer and cigarette smoke.

I'd had enough. 'Get off me!' I shouted, jumping up. 'What the hell do you think you're doing?'

He spread out his hands. 'Hey, I'm just trying to have a little fun. Don't be so uptight.'

I was at the door. 'Go to hell!' I said. I ran towards the front door. I heard him say, 'Frigid bitch', but I didn't care. I didn't care what any of them thought of me any more. I had to get out of there.

My bag was just inside the door. We'd dumped them there when we got home, in a hurry to get on with ordering the pizza and setting up the movie for the cosy girls' night in we had planned. I grabbed it, threw the door open and dashed out, slamming it behind me. I ran, not thinking about anything except getting away from that creep.

Only when I was at the end of the road, and sure that no one was following me, did I stop to take out my phone. I dialled home. Oh the blessed relief of hearing my mother's warm familiar voice.

'Mum,' I said, trying to keep my voice from shaking. 'Can you come and collect me? I want to come home.'

Dear Ellen,

If only I had told my mum everything that night. If only she had had one of her Mums Sticking Together moments and told your mum. If only your mum had come out of that fog she was living in long enough to see you were spiralling out of control. If only your dad had come home early and caught you and Pete doing whatever it is you were doing, and lost the

121

plot, and kicked him out, called the police. If only you'd been grounded for weeks and not allowed anywhere near Carrie's party. If only I'd been able to get through to you.

They just go around and around my head, these if onlys, until I want to scream and scream so loud I drown them out.

Love,

Maggie.

Five days before the party, I was dreading going into school. I hadn't heard from Ellen all day Sunday. I was still angry at her for abandoning me with that creep Spider, but also embarrassed about the fact that I'd run out of there like a little child wanting to get home to her mum.

I spent most of Sunday wondering what had happened after I left. Mostly I was hoping that Ellen's father hadn't come home and caught her, but I have to admit that part of me was hoping that he had.

I was the worst friend ever.

I didn't tell Mum what had happened. I didn't want her making a big fuss about it, I just wanted to forget the whole thing. By the time she arrived to collect me I'd managed to calm down and I just told her that I felt like I was intruding on Ellen and her dad and it was better for them to have some time alone. Mum didn't let it rest and kept quizzing me about why I hadn't waited at the house for her but I didn't tell her anything more. I'm sure she thought Ellen and I had

had a row but she probably dismissed it as just normal girl stuff.

I hung around our lockers until after the last bell had rung, hoping Ellen would show up. Finally, when the corridors had emptied, I gave up and went to English.

It was halfway through the class when Ellen sidled in. She grunted an apology in the direction of Miss Leigh, who barely acknowledged it, simply waving her to her seat. I waited to see if Ellen would look at me, but she kept her eyes firmly fixed on her book. The minute the class was over she bolted for the door.

I sighed. She was obviously annoyed at me. I didn't know what to do. It was me who should have been annoyed at her, but I hated fighting with her. And it wouldn't be the first time for me to try to smooth things over even when I knew it wasn't my fault.

I didn't get a chance to smooth things over though, because I didn't see her to speak to for the rest of the day. I don't know if she was avoiding me on purpose. I looked for her at lunch time but she was nowhere to be found – maybe she'd gone off to meet Pete again, going through the whole rigmarole of sneaking out and changing her clothes in the toilet. With a pang of jealousy I wondered if she'd asked someone else to go to the shopping centre with her. I hadn't exactly enjoyed being her cover story but it was my job and I didn't want anyone else doing it either.

It wasn't until after school that I saw her again, walking out of the gate. I was about to call out for her but then I saw that Liam was waiting for her. He took her schoolbag and the two of them walked off arm in arm.

I went home alone.

Dear Ellen,

Today I decided that I just wasn't going to speak. There's too much noise in the world as it is. I've often wished that Jamie had a mute button, and lately I'm beginning to wish Mum and Dad had one too. All that psychoanalysis from Dad and those valiant attempts to be cheerful from Mum are just exhausting to listen to. But I thought if I shut up for a while, maybe they would follow my example. Worth a try, right?

As for school, it struck me that it isn't just Carrie and Co. who've been avoiding me. I decided to see if anyone would actually talk to me if I didn't speak first. First test came as I took books out of my locker. Susan Feeney's locker is beside mine, as you know, and instead of saying hello to her as usual I said nothing. I just started taking my books out, dumping my lunch at the back and flicking through my art folder, waiting to see what she would do. She didn't ignore me completely, but really, she may as well have. She just gave me this sort of nervous smile, emptied her locker as quickly as she could, and darted off, stuffing books in her bag as she went.

Maths was first (urgh). I'd managed to get my homework

done yesterday in detention, with a bit of help from Siobhan. (Siobhan is surprisingly good at maths. Hard to believe, I know. If she wasn't so boy-crazy, I reckon she'd be quite smart, really.) Bouncer barely looked at it though. And no one else spoke to me the whole way through the class. No one asked to borrow my compass, no one slipped me a note, no one nudged me and laughed at Bouncer when he bumped his head on the desk picking up his pen from the floor. It was like I was invisible.

I wished I was invisible in geography. Old Fuddy Duddy asked me some question about volcanoes. I actually knew the answer, but I said nothing. She got impatient and repeated the question. Eventually she got fed up of me and sent me to the principal's office. Yes, me, sent to the principal. Did you ever think you'd see the day?

Mrs Carmichael couldn't manage to make me speak either, but unlike Fuddy Duddy she wasn't nasty about it. I was actually going to give in and talk because she was being so nice, but I was afraid that if I opened my mouth I'd just start to cry. In the end she phoned my mum to come and collect me.

I didn't say a word on the way home. Mum didn't either. Perhaps her attempts at being cheerful have worn her out too.

I'm in my room now. She sent me up for a lie down. It's going to be a long day. Maybe not talking isn't as good an idea as I thought.

Later,

Maggie.

Four days before the party, Ellen didn't come in to school at all.

It was our last day of proper school. The rest of the week would be taken up with end of year exams. I had that familiar sense of pre-exam panic. Why hadn't I started studying earlier? Why hadn't I done up a study plan? Why hadn't I asked Bouncer to go over quadratic equations one more time? It didn't help that we had maths first thing. What a way to start three days of exams.

It didn't make me feel any better that the exams didn't count for anything (unless you did REALLY badly, in which case it might be gently suggested to you that you drop from higher to ordinary level). I still wanted to do well.

I thought about texting Ellen, but in the end I didn't.

Dear Ellen,

My silence was the main topic of conversation at dinner today. Ha ha, how ironic. Dad said to Mum, 'Maybe we sent her back to school too soon.' Mum sighed and agreed.

Do they think I can't hear them? I'm only mute, not deaf.

Love, Maggie.

Three days before the party, Ellen came bouncing into the

126

hall as I stood at my locker looking over my notes for the first exam. Bouncer had spent most of the last week reminding us which formulas we needed to know off by heart and even though I was practically able to say them in my sleep at this stage, I was still afraid I'd forget one of the basics and not be able to do a whole question.

'Maggie, got any plans for lunchtime?'

I was so surprised that she was speaking to me as if nothing had happened that I didn't answer right away.

Ellen misunderstood my silence. 'Don't worry, I'm not going to ask you to cover for me or anything like that,' she said quickly. 'I'm not seeing Pete today, anyway. I just wondered if you wanted to go shopping for something to wear to the party on Saturday.'

'OK. I suppose we could.' I pushed my bag into my locker and shut the door. 'I was sort of planning on looking over my history notes for this afternoon, but that probably won't take long.'

'Of course not! I bet you know that history book off by heart,' Ellen said. 'I'm really glad you can come, otherwise I was going to have to ask Carrie, and she's no good. She just tells me everything looks nice on me, and then I don't know what to pick.'

I had started walking towards the gym, where the exams were on, and Ellen fell into step beside me, beginning a long ramble about the last time she'd gone shopping with Carrie, the awfulness of Carrie's taste, and how she'd nearly rather go shopping with her dad. I noticed she still had her bag with her – we weren't allowed to bring them into the gym – but maybe she was planning on leaving it in the changing room.

As we reached the corridor leading to the gym Ellen at last interrupted her own monologue to ask, 'Where are we going? It's not PE this morning, is it?'

I stared at her. 'Ellen, you do know the exams start today, don't you?'

'Really? Eek. What do we have first?'

'Maths. Please tell me you learnt those formulas Bouncer was going on about last week.'

'Hmmm. I'm not sure. It sounds kind of familiar.' She stopped to rest her bag on a windowsill and started rummaging through it unhurriedly.

'Ellen, he said we wouldn't be able to answer two of the questions without them,' I said urgently.

'I think they're in here somewhere,' Ellen murmured, still rooting around in her bag.

I checked my watch. The exam was due to start in less than five minutes. 'Look, I'll run back and get mine, they're right there in my locker. If you just look over them now I'm sure you'll be fine.'

Ellen glanced up at me. 'Give me your key, I'll go. I don't want to keep you late too,' she said, finally realising I was panicking ever so slightly.

Relieved, I handed her the key. 'It's a sheet of paper right on top of my books, you can't miss it.'

'OK. I'm gone. I'll be super fast.' She set off at a run, then shouted back to me, 'You go on, OK? Tell them I'm coming!'

I decided she was right – no point in both of us being late. I hurried towards the gym. I'd never understand Ellen. She'd always been a bit laidback about school stuff, but she'd never gone so far as to forget an exam before. Although if she could forget so quickly about what had happened on Saturday night, then it wasn't exactly surprising that she'd overlooked something so insignificant as a maths exam.

Fuddy Duddy was just handing out the test papers when Ellen arrived at the gym, out of breath, but looking quite triumphant. She'd even managed to remember to leave her bag in my locker. Along with her pencil case. I passed her a pen and pencil, ignoring Fuddy Duddy's frowns, then tried to concentrate on the first question.

Later, weeks later, Bouncer told me that Ellen had got 95% on that test. An A1, and the best mark of anyone in our year.

Dear Ellen,

Why should a person have to talk if they don't want to? Seriously, why? I don't understand it. I'm not hurting anyone. I just want to be here, silent, removed, in my own little world. Well actually that's not what I want at all. I want it to be six months ago, to be sitting in Java Bay with you, drinking pink lemonade, and giggling, and talking about everyone we can see around us, clothes, films, all the girls at school, Liam, everything, anything. Silence isn't my number one choice. Just the best one out of the options available to me.

Jamie is the only one who will just let me be. When I got home from school, he was playing with his Lego, trying to make a rocket. I sat down beside him on the floor and started to help him. He chatted away to me about rockets and engines and astronauts and aliens, and he didn't mind that I didn't answer him. We sat there for ages just building his rocket. Then Dad came home from work and asked Jamie to go and help Mum in the kitchen, but before he could leave I got up from the floor and went up to my room, closing the door behind me.

Mum came up to my room after that and begged me to talk. She started crying again. It was so embarrassing. I mean, there was no one else there, so it wasn't as bad as one of those awful public weepy scenes she's been specialising in recently, but still. It's not something I feel like dealing with right now.

I just wanted to ask her to leave, but of course I couldn't do that, because that would be giving in too, wouldn't it? So I said nothing, just sat there staring at the wall, as she pleaded and cajoled and bargained. Finally, though, it got too much for me. I climbed into bed and pulled the duvet over my head, right over, until everything was dark. That stopped her in her tracks. I lay there and listened to the silence, interrupted only by a sniff from Mum, and then, after a minute, a little sigh. I waited. Finally, finally, I heard her getting up. Footsteps. The door opening, and quietly closing again. I didn't move. I waited until I heard the sound of her boots clicking down the stairs. Then I took the duvet off, got out of bed, went over to the door, and turned the key in the lock.

I sound like a psychopath don't I?

XXX

Maggie.

Two days before the party. I stood in front of Ellen's bedroom mirror, trying on one outfit after another. Every item of clothing that Ellen owned was piled up on her bed.

I couldn't get over how many clothes Ellen had. Loads of them hadn't even been worn – the price tags were still on them.

Ellen surveyed me critically, head on one side. 'Nope. Not your colour,' she pronounced. 'Try the red. I don't know why I bought it, it looks awful with my hair.' She lifted a fistful of her red curls and grimaced.

'Was that the day you went shopping with Carrie?' I teased.

'Must have been, I think. I can't remember.'

I pulled the red top over my head. Instantly I felt transformed. I turned this way and that, admiring my reflection.

'Oh Maggie, that's perfect on you!' Ellen said.

'Do you really think so?' I asked.

'Absolutely. You have to wear it to the party.'

'Are you sure you don't mind me borrowing it?'

'Keep it,' Ellen said.

'Oh, I couldn't do that,' I began.

'Why not? I won't wear it anyway.'

I looked at myself again. It really was a lovely top. 'At least let me give you some money for it?' I said.

'No, there's no need, my dad bought it for me, it's not like it came out of my allowance or something,' Ellen said.

I started to take it off, a bit reluctantly. 'Well, thanks, it's really nice of you.'

'No problem! We have to have you looking your best on Saturday. One of those boys is bound to fall for you. Just think what a fun summer we'll have if we've both got boy-friends! We can go on double dates and everything.'

Ellen was leaning over the side of the bed looking for shoes underneath it, so she couldn't see my face, which was just as well. We still hadn't talked about what had happened last weekend. I didn't want to bring it up, and Ellen seemed to have forgotten all about it.

'Oh, do you think there'll be any nice guys there?' I asked, turning away before she reappeared from under the bed and pretending to look through her make-up bag.

'I think Liam's bringing some of the football team,' Ellen said. 'Oh, that reminds me. I said we'd go to the cinema tomorrow night with Liam. A sort of early end of exams celebration, since the party's not until Saturday. Carrie and Stephanie said they might go too. My dad's taking us out for dinner first, but I said I'd meet Liam after that.'

'Sounds great, but I'm not sure Mum will let me go out two nights in a row,' I said.

'I'll ask her for you,' Ellen promised. 'I'll make sure to tell her how hard you've been working! You have to come, Liam said he'd bring his mate Sean. You can suss him out, see if you like him – then make your move at the party!'

'Ellen, what are you like?' I laughed. 'I don't even know the guy.' And anyway it wouldn't matter, I added silently, since there was only one boy I wanted.

'Exactly, so tomorrow is your chance to get to know him!' Ellen said. 'I can't believe the exams are over tomorrow, I can't wait!'

'Oh, because you spent so much time studying,' I laughed.

Ellen threw a shoe at me. It missed, but it did knock a pile of clothes off the mirror. Soon we were throwing everything at each other, her room was an even bigger mess than before, piles everywhere, clothes all over the place, and even a random shoe on top of her dressing table. We were laughing so hard we could hardly breathe.

Dear Ellen,

My room is so peaceful. I'd forgotten what it's like to just spend time in here, quietly, all alone. When you disappeared first I spent a lot of time in here, but it didn't help. I felt trapped, cooped up, unable to breathe. I wanted to be out there looking for you, doing something, but no one seemed to want my help.

Now my room is a refuge, and I don't mind that I'm not out doing something, because I have come to realise there is nothing I can do except wait.

I love that my room is a mixture of all the mes that there have been. Mostly of course it's the current me. Huge desk, which I keep pretty neat and tidy, most of the time anyway. There's a pile of books in one corner, lots of stationery (I love stationery) – coloured paper clips, fancy pens collected over the years in different places I've visited, stampers, my folder with lots of different kinds of paper. My computer. My folders from school.

Above my desk, there are some sketches I've done of different fashion ideas. Some of them are awful – what was I thinking? But some of them, the newer ones, are actually quite good. Maybe even good enough to put in my portfolio for applying to art college when the time comes.

Over my bed is a print of Hell by Hieronymus Bosch. My mother hates it. She grimaces every time she looks at it. I can see her biting her tongue so as not to say something. The downside of encouraging your children to express themselves is sometimes their self-expression isn't quite to your taste, eh Mum?

Underneath Hieronymus Bosch, there's a bit of wallpaper from my Disney Princesses phase which my dad didn't bother stripping off when we did up my room a few years ago. It was such a pain taking it all off, he was relieved when I said not to bother with that bit as my poster would be going on top. And where Snow White is peeling away, you can just see Winnie the Pooh, and a bit of Tigger, from when this wasn't a bedroom but a nursery. All the layers of my life, there on a wall for anyone to see, if they know where to look.

The bookshelves are crammed. Art books. Fashion books. Thrillers. All my **Malory Towers** books which I still like to read sometimes, when I'm sick or when I just can't be bothered with anything more grown-up. And on the top shelf are all the cuddly toys which I can't bear to give away or even put in the attic.

Then there's my sewing machine, and my chair piled high with about ten different sewing projects at various different stages of completeness. I haven't felt much like working on any of them lately, but it's good to know they're there.

I love my room. It's me. And it's you too. The pink teddy you won at a funfair and insisted on giving to me. The jewellery box you gave me once for my birthday, with a ballet dancer who twirls around and around when you open the lid. The photo on the shelf of the two of us at the ice skating rink, all scarves and gloves and hats, our cheeks rosy from the cold, and the biggest smiles on our faces. The stars on the ceiling which glow in the dark. We used to lie in bed and count them,

and you used to pretend you could see all the different con-
stellations, and tease me that I couldn't, and then tease me
again for believing you.

I don't want to leave my room, and go back out into that
world that doesn't have you in it.

Love,

Maggie.

Amazingly, Mum said yes, as long as it was just the cinema,
and that she would be there to collect me as soon as the film
was over. She dropped me off with her usual list of instructions. I waited until she was gone before rolling my eyes at
her, which only made me feel slightly better.

Liam was sitting on a wall outside the cinema. He smiled
when he saw me coming. 'Hi Maggie. What's up?'

'Oh, the usual. So relieved to have the exams over,' I said.
I leaned against the wall beside him, careful not to stand too
close.

'How did they go?'

'Not too bad,' I said. 'Well, maths was a bit of a nightmare,
and I didn't really like the Irish paper, but the others weren't
too bad. How about you?'

'Same – maths was a disaster,' Liam said, shaking his head.
'I'm just no good at it.'

Carrie and Stephanie arrived, and then Liam's friend Sean,
but there was still no sign of Ellen.

Liam checked his watch. 'The film is starting in a couple of minutes. Wonder where Ellen's got to?'

'I'll give her a ring,' I said.

'We'll go on in,' Carrie said. 'No point all of us missing the start of the film.' She, Stephanie and Sean headed into the cinema.

I dialled Ellen's number, but it rang out. Liam had made no move to follow the others.

'You go ahead too, I can wait for Ellen,' I said.

'No, it's OK. I'd better make sure she's all right,' Liam said.

Just then there was a roar of a car engine with the silencer removed. Pete's – of course. Ellen got out of the back seat, half falling and grabbing another car nearby to steady herself. The car was full of Pete's mates – one of them banged the door behind Ellen. Pete drove off without even checking she was all right. I rushed over to her but Liam got there first.

'Are you OK?' he demanded, taking her by the arm.

Ellen pushed her hair out of her face, swaying slightly as she straightened up. 'Never better. What did I miss?'

'How much have you had to drink?' Liam demanded.

'What are you, my father?' Ellen said. 'Oh wait no, because he couldn't actually care less about me.'

Liam guided her over to the low wall outside the cinema and helped her sit down. I sat on the other side of her and asked, 'Did something happen with your dad?'

'Useless jerk,' Ellen said. 'He was supposed to take Robert

and me out for dinner this evening but he cancelled at the last minute. He said some work thing had come up, but I know it's just another lie. He didn't even ring, he just sent me a text, and then when I told Robert he was devastated, he started crying and screaming at me as if it was my fault.'

'You poor thing. You should have phoned me,' I said.

'Pete said he'd take me out and cheer me up,' Ellen said. 'We went back to his place for a while, but the band are heading off somewhere so I said I'd come and meet you guys instead.'

'Come on, let's go and see the film,' Liam said. 'Don't let him ruin your evening.'

'Think it might be too late!' Ellen said. 'Go on then, we may as well.'

'Can you manage to act sober long enough for us to get tickets?' I asked.

'I'll hold her up!' Liam joked. He put his arm around her waist and she leaned into him. I turned away.

We couldn't find the others so the three of us ended up sitting on our own at the back. The film was a rom-com and not too demanding, which was just as well, as it was hard to concentrate. Ellen ignored it completely, obsessively checking her phone for texts and muttering under her breath. A couple of times I saw her take a swig out of a naggin of vodka she had stashed in her pocket. I glanced around anxiously, wondering if anyone was watching her. If someone told the staff what she was doing we could all be thrown out. I looked over at Liam and he just grimaced, as if to say we should just let it go.

I don't even know what the film was about – whatever bit of my mind wasn't occupied in worrying about Ellen was kind of overwhelmed by the fact that I was there, at the cinema, with Liam, even though there was a drunken Ellen and a jumbo bucket of popcorn in between us.

A couple of rows in front of us, I saw a buxom blonde edging past people as she returned to her seat from the bathroom. I watched her, glad to have something else to think about for a moment. The man she was with turned to kiss her as she sat down. I realised with a shock that it was Ellen's dad – and the blonde could be none other than the Homewrecker.

I tried to distract Ellen by knocking over the popcorn. 'Oh no, I'm so sorry,' I exclaimed. But it was too late. Ellen was staring in disbelief at her father.

'What the hell?' she shouted. People in front of us turned around and shushed her.

'Ellen, it's OK,' I said, trying to take her arm. She shook me off.

'Do you see him?' she demanded.

'Yes, I know,' I said, conscious of all the eyes on us.

'He said he was going to a bloody meeting!' she said, making absolutely no attempt to keep her voice down.

'What's going on?' Liam whispered.

'It's her dad,' I told him. 'He's up there with his girlfriend.'

Mr Barrett didn't turn around, but I'm sure he must have heard her, because it seemed like everyone in the cinema could. I tried to calm Ellen down.

'He's a jerk, OK? He's not worth wasting your time on,' I said.

'He's my dad,' she said, her face crumbling. She kicked the seat in front of her really hard. The woman sitting there turned around again and said, 'Do you mind?!'

'Yes I do bloody mind actually,' Ellen shouted at her. 'I'm sick of this!'

'So leave then,' the woman told her. 'The rest of us want to watch the film.'

A flashlight shone in our eyes. I recognised the guy from the ticket counter.

'I'm going to have to ask you to leave,' he said, looking at me though it clearly wasn't me he meant.

'It's OK, we're going,' I said. Liam was talking to Ellen, trying to get her to calm down, and the two of us led her out of the row. I mumbled an apology to the ticket guy, staring at the ground in front of us to avoid the curious eyes all turned in our direction as we walked down the aisle.

Outside, Ellen suddenly broke away from us and ran down the steps into the car park. A car had to brake suddenly to avoid hitting her, but she took no notice.

'There's his bloody car,' she yelled, still running. 'His bloody car that he cares about more than me and Robert, because he thinks he can impress the bloody Homewrecker.'

She ran towards her dad's car and I saw her pulling her keys out of her pocket. I was running after her, trying desperately to reach her before she did something really stupid, but Liam got there before me. He grabbed her arm just as she was about to drag the keys along the shiny silver paintwork of the BMW.

'Let go of me!' Ellen screeched, but Liam held her firmly, taking her other hand too to stop her hitting him.

'Ellen, you have to calm down,' he told her. 'Do you want to get arrested?'

'Hey, what's going on?' It was the guy who'd thrown us out of the cinema, standing on the front steps looking down at us. 'Get away from that car before I call the guards!'

Liam let go of Ellen. The cinema guy started running down the steps but Ellen was faster, hopping over the wall. We took off after her. This time she managed not to run into the speeding traffic, dodging round a corner and heading off down a side street.

She managed to shake off not just the cinema guy (who wasn't even following her anyway – he'd given up once we were off the cinema property) but us too – as we came around a corner there was no sign of her. I stopped, out of breath – I hadn't run that much in ages. Liam waited for me, anxiously scouring the street.

'Where did she go?' I said.

We walked on down the street, looking into shops and down side streets, but there was no sign of her. At the end of the road we decided to turn back and look again. I thought she couldn't have got far and we must have just missed her somehow.

'God, not again,' Liam said. He pointed to an off-licence across the road. Ellen had joined the queue at the till, a large bottle of vodka in her hands.

Liam headed across the road and I followed, taking one last look behind to make sure no one else was coming after us. When I got inside Liam was already arguing with Ellen and trying to take the bottle out of her hands.

'Get lost, will you?' Ellen hissed at him. 'You're embarrassing me.'

'Forget it, mate. I'm not serving her anyway,' the guy behind the counter said.

'What do you mean?' Ellen demanded. 'I'm eighteen.'

'Where's your ID then?' he asked, in a bored tone.

Ellen pretended to rummage in her bag, muttering, 'I know I had it in here somewhere.'

The guy jerked his thumb in the direction of the door. 'Beat it, kids. I've had the guards in here twice already this week. I'm not risking my licence to serve a couple of snotty-nosed teenagers.'

Liam tried to pull Ellen in the direction of the door. She suddenly stopped resisting and made a dash for the door – the bottle of vodka still in her hands.

'Oi!' the guy yelled. 'Get back here!' He lifted up the counter to let himself out.

'It's OK, I'll stop her,' I said quickly, not wanting him to go after her – God knows what she would do.

'You'd better, or I'll call the guards,' he said, heading after her all the same.

'Already called them,' said a voice from the back of the shop. An older man, probably the manager, was standing there with the phone in his hand.

Liam had managed to wrestle the bottle off Ellen. She took off again and he shoved it at me before running after her. I handed it to the guy in the shop with a totally inadequate 'Sorry!' and ran after the others. I heard a police siren wailing in the background. Oh God, surely they weren't sending a car out after us?

I caught up with Ellen and Liam just inside the park. All attempts at bravado had failed her and she was crying quietly, Liam's arm around her. We sat down on the nearest bench, both of us putting our arms around her now and just letting her cry.

'Well, there's a night out we won't forget in a hurry,' Liam joked.

'It's never boring with Ellen around, that's for sure,' I said.

Ellen said nothing, just leaned against Liam's shoulder, mascara running down her cheeks. We sat there for what seemed like ages, Liam and I talking about stupid things, trying to get Ellen to cheer up or at least say something, but it was like she wasn't really hearing us at all.

'Think we'd better get you home,' Liam said at last.

'Sounds like a good idea,' said a voice behind us.

I looked up to see a guard standing over us. He wasn't that old, maybe twenty-three or four, and he was tall and good-looking. Under normal circumstances I might have fancied him, but these circumstances were about as far from normal as you could get.

'I've had reports of some youngsters involved in a row outside the cinema,' the guard said.

We said nothing. Liam and I just stared at him, waiting to see what he would say next, and Ellen looked at the ground.

'And there was an incident at an off-licence – a minor attempting to purchase alcohol, and then attempting to shop-lift,' the guard continued. There was a long pause before he added, 'But you wouldn't know anything about that, would you?'

'No, guard,' Liam said quickly. 'Nothing to do with us.'

The guard squatted down in front of the bench, looking at each of us in turn. 'The owner of the off-licence tells me he has it all on CCTV footage. A young lady with red hair, I believe.' He stared pointedly at Ellen's hair.

Oh God. A hundred things flashed through my mind. Being arrested. My parents being hauled in to the garda station. Ellen's mum and dad screaming at each other. Being in the local paper.

'I'm sure we can sort this all out,' the guard said, his tone surprisingly gentle. 'Anything you'd like to tell me?'

I looked desperately at Liam and amazingly he came to the rescue of us all. 'There may have been a little incident at the off-licence,' he said. 'But we didn't mean it, honestly. She was just letting off a bit of steam – we've just finished our exams. I dared her to go in, but we weren't really going to steal anything.'

I wondered if the guard would buy it. He seemed to think for a long time, before straightening up. 'Well, it seems no harm was done this time,' he said slowly.

'No, and it won't happen again,' Liam assured him.

'It better not,' the guard said. 'I'll be keeping an eye out for you. This is a small town you know.' But his tone was kinder than his words, and he added, 'How are you getting home?'

'My mum is picking us up,' I said, only realising as I said it that it must be nearly time for her to arrive.

'Are you sure now? I don't want to give any of your parents heart attacks by dropping you home in the squad car,' he said, a twinkle in his eye.

'It's fine, honestly, guard,' Liam said. 'I'll make sure they get home OK. We're going to meet her mum now.'

'Well, just make sure that you do,' the guard said. He seemed about to leave, then stopped to say, 'I'm Declan, by the way. Just in case you get arrested and need someone to rescue you.' He turned away, with Liam and me both mumbling our thanks.

Throughout this whole thing Ellen had said absolutely nothing. We persuaded her to get to her feet and start walking with us back towards the cinema. I let Liam look after her, hanging back a little to send a text to my mum, asking her to pick us up at the ice cream parlour around the corner. I thought it was probably better not to bring Ellen within sight of the cinema again.

I told Liam what I'd done, but he said, 'Maybe I should just take Ellen home in a taxi. Your mum will go nuts if she sees her like this. There's no point getting her into trouble when we've managed to get off so lightly so far.'

I realised he was right. I hugged Ellen and said goodbye to them both at the taxi rank. I walked the final few yards to the ice cream parlour, turning back to watch as Liam held the taxi door open for her and gently helped her into the car.

I sat down at a table outside to wait on my own.

Dear Ellen,

We were so stupid, Liam and me. We thought we were doing the right thing for you, the thing friends do. Maybe if we'd been real friends to you none of this would have happened.

David says that's not true and none of this is my fault, but I'm finding it hard to believe him.

Love,

Maggie.

I woke up the next morning, the day of the party, wondering if all those things had really happened or if it had just been some kind of bad dream. I checked my phone. There was a text from Liam, wondering if I'd heard from Ellen, but nothing from her. I tried to phone her but it just rang out. She was probably just sleeping off her hangover.

I spent the day mooching around the house, helping Mum with bits and pieces of housework and Jamie with his Lego. It was weird not to have any studying to do. I kept trying Ellen until she eventually sent me a text saying she was fine and that she was going out with Pete. I hoped he was going to take better care of her than he had the day before.

At last it was time to get ready for the party. I wished Ellen was there – we always got ready for nights out together.

My phone rang as I was just finishing my make-up. Ellen's name flashed up on the screen. I scrutinised my face in the mirror. Had I overdone it on the eye shadow? Mum would say yes. Ellen would say I wasn't wearing enough. I decided I would do. 'Hey, Ellen, what's up?'

'Maggie, there's been a change of plan.'

Oh no. Not again. 'Ellen you promised, you absolutely

swore …'

'Chill out, Maggie, I'm still going OK? I'll just meet you there instead.'

'What's happened? Why can't I come with you?'

'Pete's going to drive me. I'd get him to collect you too, but he's got the rest of the band with him, and I know your mum wouldn't want you piling in with another seven people!'

She'd got that one right, anyway. My mum would never stand back and watch me get into a car where I wouldn't have a seatbelt. I don't think she was quite over the fact that they didn't make car seats for the over twelves. Anyway, there was no way I would want to get into a car where I might end up being squashed up beside Spider.

'OK, I guess I can ask Mum to bring me. What time are you going to be there?'

'I'm not sure. As soon as I can, OK?'

'Will I wait for you outside?'

Ellen laughed. 'No, don't be daft, just go on in. It's just going to be people from school, right? I think Pete will be the most exotic person there!'

'OK.' She knew I hated going into places like that alone, she bloody knew it.

'Gotta go. I'll see you there, OK?'

She hung up abruptly, and I was left staring at my own reflection. The party hadn't even started, and already I felt like the night was going all wrong.

I reached for a wipe and scrubbed off all the eye shadow.

Dear Ellen,

I'm sorry I haven't written in a while. And now I feel silly for saying that, because what difference does it make to you?

The truth is, I've been engaged in another battle, with my mum, the school, the world at large you could say. My mum got David to pay a home visit. Normally he doesn't do that. I go to his office, which is very nice. It's on the second floor of this tall narrow building, above a shop and a dental surgery, and you have to go up a narrow stairway to get to it. I try to shut out the sound of the dentist's drill, or that horrible cleaning machine, when I'm going past the surgery. It's always a relief to get to David's floor and see his nice smiling receptionist, who always remembers my name, and says something nice about my clothes or my hair as she shows me into David's room.

David's room is quite big, with a huge window looking out over the park. He doesn't have any pictures, just all his certificates and things in frames on the wall, and shelves filled with books. There's a brown leather couch. The first time I got there, I asked him if I was supposed to lie on it, and he grinned and said only if I wanted to, that most people just preferred one of the armchairs beside the fireplace. Mostly it was just when whole families came in together that he used the couch. So I sat on the armchair facing towards the

149

window, and when I was talking, and didn't feel like looking at him, I looked past him, out the window, and tried to spot shapes in the clouds.

Anyway, like I said, he came to see me. My mother brought him up to my room. He was very friendly, as he always is, making jokes and taking no notice of the fact that I wasn't joining in. Actually, he was pretty sneaky about that. Like when he looked at one of my sketches, he said, 'This is really good. It looks like you might have done it.' He didn't ask me a question, so it didn't matter that I wasn't answering him. He went to the window then, and admired the garden. He said he wished he had that much space, but he and his wife just had a small patch of garden, and no side entrance because they are in the middle of a terrace. He said his wife had green fingers, and every summer their garden was filled with colour, but that he would really like to have more space so that they could have some trees.

It was weird hearing him talking so much actually. In his office I do most of the talking, and he only speaks when he asks me a question, or to encourage me to say something more. He never talks about himself. I didn't even know he was married.

Then he came and sat down at my desk, and put his hands together, resting on his knees. He looked at me with this kind but serious expression and started to talk about how what I'm experiencing is denial, which is one of the stages

150

of grief, when a person disappears from our lives, in whatever way that happens. He said it's natural to wallow in denial for a while (that's the word he used – wallow – which always makes me think of pigs) but that I mustn't let it take over my life. He talked about what Ellen would want me to do, which was to think of her, but to keep doing the things I enjoyed, and the things I didn't enjoy but that needed to be done – school, homework, chores. General engagement with the world.

That made me feel a bit cross, because he didn't know Ellen, so how could he know what she would want me to do? But I didn't have time to dwell on that, because then he was talking about a place I could go for a while to have a bit of time to clear my head. He mentioned having counselling sessions every day, and group therapy sessions, talking to other teenagers who've been through a tough time too, and he said I'd have my own room, and plenty of time to be alone, but with someone always on hand if I needed them. But I knew that what he was talking about was walls, and doors with alarms on them, and being watched all the time, and I shook my head, and when he persisted I said, 'No!'. And I was surprised at the sound of my own voice, which was a bit scratchy, as if maybe rust had grown on it when it wasn't being used. And David was surprised too, and he smiled and said, 'No one's going to make you go Maggie, but if you won't talk to me or your family then you're making it very hard for us to help you'.

'I will talk,' I said. I hated myself for giving in so easily, but I hated the thought of being sent away even more.

'That's good Maggie. I'm glad to hear that. You can tell me whatever you want and it will be completely confidential. You know that don't you?'

I said nothing. Just because I had agreed to talk didn't mean I felt like doing it right now. David seemed to know this, and didn't try to push me. He waited a moment then asked, 'How are you getting on with that diary you're writing? Well not a diary as such, I know, but an account of what happened.'

I said nothing again. The truth was that I had reached the point I was most dreading, that I simply didn't want to recall, and I wasn't sure when I would be able to face it.

'I hope it's been a help, writing it all down,' David said. 'If you want to show it to me, I'd be happy to read it. Sometimes it's easier than talking.'

'OK,' I said. 'Not yet, though.'

David smiled. He stood up. 'Well, I think I'd better be getting home. Helen's rustling up some fajitas for dinner. My favourite.'

He made his way to the door. 'So, I'll see you again on Tuesday, right? I'm going to tell your mother to let you stay off school until then. Hopefully on Wednesday you might feel up to going into the big bad world again and using that nice little voice of yours'. He hesitated a moment, then said, 'Do try to write some more if you can. Ellen would want you to. Maybe there'll be something that will help you make sense of why she did what she did.'

I watched him go, heard him clattering down the stairs and into the kitchen to talk to Mum, and I felt irritated again that he was presuming to know what Ellen would think, but mostly I felt cross because I knew that he was right.

Love,

Maggie.

I could hear Carrie's party before I even saw her house. It's just as well there's an old lady who's mostly deaf on one side of her, and a guy who works night shifts and is never home on the other, because otherwise her parents would be getting an irate phone call or two the next day. The music was so loud the house was practically vibrating. I stood on the doorstep, feeling nervous. I hated going in to parties on my own, not knowing if I'd have someone to talk to. I couldn't believe Ellen had let me down.

I glanced down at my red top and felt a bit more confident – it really was lovely, Ellen had fabulous taste. And she was right too about the jeans and ballet flats. Not too dressy, but not too casual either.

Could anyone even hear me ringing the doorbell? I couldn't hear it from outside, but whether that was because it wasn't working, or because of the squeals and general mayhem inside, I wasn't sure.

I was just pressing my nose up against the glass to look into the hall when the door opened and I stumbled in. Oh great, just the classy entrance I was hoping for.

'Maggie, I can't believe you've been drinking already, that's so not like you!' Carrie squealed, pulling me into the hall. 'Where's Ellen?'

'She's coming a bit later,' I said.

'She'd better, everyone's dying to meet the band. Plus the guy to girl ratio is all wrong!' Carrie was screeching into my ear, and I couldn't help recoiling from her beer breath. She laughed as if she'd just said something hilarious. It looked as if she was the one who'd overdone it already.

'Go into the kitchen, grab yourself a drink … oh look, more party people, hurray!' She made a dive for the door.

Right. Kitchen. I'd been in this house a million times, but it looked weirdly different. Carrie had closed all the blinds and replaced the ordinary white light bulbs with red and blue ones. The result was almost cave-like – I felt like I was heading into the centre of the earth as I made my way to the kitchen.

The first person I saw was Siobhan Brady. Wearing a very short black dress and stiletto heels that made her look at least five years older, she was perched on the kitchen table surrounded by Jacci and the rest of her faithful followers. She seemed to be in the middle of some story and the other girls were hanging on her every word.

I was about to just back quietly out of the kitchen, but Siobhan spotted me.

'Hey Maggie. All alone tonight? Where's her majesty?'

I said nothing. I wasn't going to get sucked into Siobhan Brady's little mind games.

'Hey, I'm just kidding. I don't know why you waste your time on Ellen anyway. She's such a loser.'

The other girls tittered appreciatively.

'She's my friend,' I said quietly.

'Where is she then?' Siobhan demanded. 'Carrie said you were getting a lift with her.'

'There was a change of plan. She's coming later.'

I looked towards the doorway, hoping Carrie would come in and rescue me, but she was ushering a gang of new arrivals into the sitting room.

Siobhan slowly got down from the table and detached herself from the group. She towered above me in the heels.

'You're wasting your time with Ellen,' she repeated. 'She's a drunk and a slapper.' Putting her face right next to mine, she lowered her voice and said into my ear, 'And you should hear the things she's been saying about you behind your back.'

Siobhan smelt like heavy perfume and something alcoholic. I resisted the temptation to pull away from her. 'Like what?'

A nasty smile crossed her face. 'Oh, just little things. Like how you're a complete walkover and you drop everything when she clicks her fingers.'

'You're lying,' I snapped, but even as I said it I felt a cold fear deep inside. I WAS a walkover; I did drop everything when Ellen wanted me to – but did other people see me that way? Did ELLEN see me that way and repeat it to other people? I always just thought she was thoughtless, but what if she was really just using me and laughing about me behind my back?

'Ask anyone,' Siobhan said, indicating the other girls with a casual wave of her hand.

'Oh, like your little groupies are going to say anything different,' I said, my voice shaking in spite of myself.

Siobhan shrugged gracefully, making the silver beads of her necklace clack against each other. 'Believe what you want Maggie, I'm just trying to give you a friendly warning.'

I'd heard enough. I turned and fled out of the kitchen in search of the only safe refuge at parties – the bathroom. But there was someone in the main bathroom, and three other girls I didn't know were waiting outside.

By now the tears were flowing down my cheeks and I couldn't stop them. One of the girls waiting on the stairs stared at me, and I turned away. I needed to be on my own.

Carrie's parents' bedroom was always off limits for parties, but I hoped maybe she had forgotten to lock the door. I tried the handle and was so relieved when it turned. I slipped inside and locked the door behind me, then rushed into the en suite and locked that too.

I stared at myself in the mirror. Just as well I had taken off the mascara or it would be running down my cheeks by now. I looked such a mess as it was. Taking a few deep breaths, I splashed some cold water on my cheeks and tried to get rid of the redness. I found some powder in my bag and put it all over my face.

I stood up on the toilet seat and looked out the tiny window, hoping to see Pete's car, but there was no sign of it. I took out my phone and sent Ellen a text saying, 'Where are you?'

I waited a while but there was no answer. I knew I couldn't stay in the bathroom all night, but I really didn't feel like facing Siobhan again.

Right. Deep breath. I'd just keep away from Siobhan. There were enough people at the party that I wouldn't have to see her anyway. Maybe Liam would be there.

I opened the door of the en suite and immediately realised there was someone banging on the bedroom door. My heart sank.

'Who the hell is in there? It's off limits!'

Eeek – it was Jane, Carrie's big sister. She was seventeen, and was usually to be found hovering in the background at Carrie's parties, keeping an eye on things.

I opened the door cautiously. 'Sorry, Jane. There was a queue for the bathroom. I didn't think you'd mind.'

'Oh it's only you – that's OK then. Come out quickly, I want to lock the door before anyone gets any ideas.'

Carrie appeared behind her. 'The way Tara is snogging Jack I reckon they'll be looking for a room any minute,' she giggled.

Jane pulled the door closed behind me and turned the key in the lock. She put the key in her pocket. 'Oh God, I think there's someone in my room too. It better not be Tara and Jack – Mum would freak.'

She rushed off to investigate, leaving me and Carrie alone.

'Where has Ellen got to? I thought she'd be here by now,' Carrie said.

'So did I,' I told her.

'I hope she's still coming. I've been telling everyone about Pete and the band. Come on, let's go down to the sitting room.'

Carrie stumbled on the stairs and I grabbed her arm to steady her. I wondered just how much she'd had to drink, and if Jane knew.

We got downstairs and Carrie said she was going to get another drink, so I ended up going into the sitting room on my own. I didn't ask her if Liam was there. I wanted to see him, but I didn't want anyone to know that I did.

Who WERE all these people? This was supposed to be an end of term party, but apart from Siobhan and Co. I hadn't seen anyone from school. I recognised Carrie's cousin Tara by her blonde hair – the rest of her was buried underneath the guy who was snogging her on the couch. Another couple were similarly occupied in the armchair by the fireplace, and a gang of boys were crowded around on the window seat drinking cans of beer and shouting to make themselves heard over the thumping music. I looked desperately around for someone to talk to, but the boys were the only ones not engaged in exchanging saliva, and there was no way I was walking up to a group of boys I didn't know. Oh, God.

Just then I felt a hand on my elbow. 'Hey, Maggie.'

It was Liam. I'd never been so glad to see him in my life.

'How's it going?' he asked.

'So far it pretty much sucks,' I said. 'Carrie's running around like a headless chicken, Jane's panicking over people getting into the bedrooms, Siobhan's bitching away as usual and Ellen's not here yet.'

Liam grinned. 'Not quite the night out you were expecting then. My useless friends aren't here yet either. Let's go out to the garden will we? It's a bit quieter.'

I was only too glad to agree.

I wondered if anyone would see us (me and Liam. Together. Alone.), but there was no one who knew us in a position to take any notice. We passed Carrie who appeared to be throwing up in the downstairs toilet. Jane was holding her hair back and scolding.

The kitchen was now jammed and I couldn't see Siobhan

anywhere, much to my relief. Liam held the back door open for me. Jacci and a few other girls were standing on the patio smoking, but they took no notice of us. Liam ushered me down to the back of the garden where there was a bench tucked away in a corner. A trellis, covered in ivy and purple clematis, hid it from view of the house.

My heart was beating so fast it actually hurt. I couldn't believe this was actually happening. I had imagined this moment so many times, being alone with Liam – him *choosing* to be alone with me – and now I didn't know what to say, could not begin to acknowledge to myself what I wanted to happen.

Liam was quiet too. I sat down on the bench, but he stayed standing, leaning against the trellis and studying one of the large purple flowers as if he was trying to count the number of petals. I smoothed my top down over my jeans and examined my fingernails.

Eventually Liam spoke, but it wasn't exactly what I wanted to hear. 'So what are we going to do about Ellen?'

I felt a sinking sensation in my stomach. Oh God, I was such an idiot. Here I was thinking it was me he wanted to be with, and all the time he just wanted to get me on my own so he could talk about Ellen. I was absolutely mortified and felt grateful he wasn't looking at me just then, because I was sure my face must be on fire. Thank God I hadn't said anything.

I tried to focus. 'I don't know,' I said. 'She just won't listen.'

'Is she coming later?'

'She's supposed to be. Pete is giving her a lift.'

Liam's face darkened. 'That jerk. I don't know what she's doing with him. I can't believe he just dropped her off at the cinema last night when she was so upset.'

'I know.' I stared into the distance, blinking hard to try to stop the tears that were building up. It was hard to concentrate on what he was saying because it was so different from what I'd been stupid enough to hope for.

'Do you think her mum has any idea what's going on?' Liam asked. 'She was already in bed when I took Ellen home.'

'Her mum is not exactly with it at the moment,' I said. 'I mean, with the separation and everything, she's got a lot on her plate.'

'If that was my sister hanging around with someone like Pete my mum would hit the roof,' Liam said.

He sat down beside me. It was a small bench, so there wasn't a lot of space. I was painfully aware of his jeans touching against mine, but I didn't want to move.

'She's lucky to have a friend like you,' Liam said softly. He was gazing at me now. I wanted to look somewhere, anywhere, but at him, but I couldn't tear my eyes away. A lock of hair fell over his forehead and I longed to reach up and brush it away.

Suddenly Liam's hand was on my face, his fingers lightly

brushing along my jawline. I was frozen to the spot, gazing up into his big brown eyes.

'I just wish …' Liam let the sentence trail off, still touching my face. I could hardly breathe.

'There you are!'

It was Ellen, her voice harsh, accusatory. Liam immediately took his hand away and sat back.

'What are you two up to?' Ellen demanded.

'Nothing,' I stammered.

'I've been looking for you everywhere, Maggie,' Ellen said.

'Well you can't have been looking for that long,' I said. 'I've been all over the house in the last twenty minutes, and we only came out to the garden about two minutes ago.'

'Oh sorry … did I interrupt your little tête-à-tête?' Ellen said snidely. 'Want me to go away so you can pick up where you left off?'

'It's not like that, Ellen,' Liam said, standing up.

'What's it like then?' she demanded. 'Tell me, because it seems pretty obvious to me.'

'What do you care anyway?' Liam said.

'I don't.' Ellen turned as if to storm off. He put out a hand to stop her. 'Ellen, we're worried about you. We both are.'

Her eyes flickered from him to me and back again. 'Well, don't be. I don't need you two acting like some sort of over-protective mother hens. I've already got two parents breathing down my neck all the time.'

162

'If that was true we wouldn't be so worried,' I said. 'I suppose they have no idea what happened last night.'

'No, why would they?' Ellen said. 'Unless you want to run off telling tales to them.'

'Ellen, that's not fair,' Liam said. I felt a small thrill that he was sticking up for me. 'It's thanks to Maggie and me that you didn't get arrested last night.'

'God, the two of you are so boring, would you ever just live a little?' Ellen said. 'So what if I got arrested, it's like a rite of passage, isn't it?'

Liam held up his hands as if to say he gave up. 'Fine, next time I won't bother, see how you like the inside of a police cell.'

'Oh, get over yourself,' Ellen snapped. She turned and stormed off back towards the house.

I looked at Liam but he just shook his head and walked off after her. I stayed where I was for a few minutes, thinking I'd better let Liam talk to her alone for a few minutes.

When I went back in the party seemed to have taken on a totally different vibe. Pete and the band had taken over the sitting room and replaced Dancing Queen with some sort of heavy metal rubbish. Pete was drinking one of Carrie's beers, and one of the other guys was offering his naggin of vodka to any passing girls. The party, which had been a bit messy but still definitely teenage, had become something else, and I felt an unexplained but real sense of fear.

Then I saw Spider. He was sitting on the edge of an armchair leaning over some girl, whispering into her ear. He moved his head back for a moment, and I saw that it was Carrie, looking pale and exhausted after her sickness bout.

I left the room, looking for Ellen. I had wanted to try to explain that there was nothing going on with Liam and me, but now I was back to being really angry with her.

I found her in the kitchen, helping herself to beers from the fridge.

'I can't believe you, Ellen,' I said.

'What now?'

She pushed the fridge door shut with her hip, cradling her bottles of beer.

'How could you invite that creep?'

'What are you talking about?'

'You know what I'm talking about. He's in there now, leching all over Carrie.'

Her face relaxed. 'Oh you mean Spider. So what? Just because you weren't interested doesn't mean Carrie isn't.'

'Carrie is completely hammered. She doesn't have a clue what she's doing.'

'Well, she's got her big sister here to look after her, she doesn't need you as well. Look, the guys are waiting for their beers. I'll come back and talk to you in a minute, OK?'

I followed her into the hall, hanging back as she went into the sitting room. I waited, but she didn't come back.

Jane was sweeping up glass that someone had smashed. I went to give her a hand. She pushed her hair out of her face and I saw that there were tears in her eyes. 'This party is getting out of hand, Maggie. My parents are going to freak out if there's any more damage done. Some of those jerks that Ellen brought have started a darts competition only they're using one of my dad's paintings as a dartboard. And I have no idea where Carrie is.'

'She's in the sitting room. Actually, she could probably do with being rescued,' I said. I told her, as briefly as I could, about Spider. She handed me the dust pan and rushed off without another word.

I felt really sorry for Jane, and furious with Ellen that she could ruin everything by bringing those awful guys to the party. Why were we, her old friends, not enough for her any more? I finished sweeping up the broken glass and went out the back to empty the dust pan into the bin. I couldn't see Liam anywhere.

What was I doing at this party? I thought longingly of my room, and my comfy bed, and the mystery novel I was reading.

Ellen came out of the sitting room. 'Jane has got her knickers in a knot.'

'Can you blame her?' I snapped.

'We're leaving. Remember that party I was telling you about? One of the band's mates?'

I just stared at her.

'You can come too, Maggie. I want you to come. So does Pete, he asked for you especially.'

'Where is it?' I found myself saying, even though I had no intention of going, not even if it was right next door.

Ellen named a village about twenty miles away. 'It's OK, Pete's got the car, he's going to drive us all. Please say you'll come.'

'No Ellen, I can't, and I don't think you should go either. Pete's been drinking. It's not safe for him to drive.'

'He's fine. He's only had one or two.'

'What about getting home?'

'Dave said we can stay the night. Crash on the sofa or whatever. Pete will be fine to drive by morning. Well probably lunchtime!'

'Won't your mum freak out if you're not home?'

'I told her I was staying over at your place. Why don't you ring your mum now, say you're staying at mine?'

She really had thought of everything. Except how I was going to feel.

'No,' I said softly. 'I don't think so.'

'Oh come on, Maggie, what's the worst thing that can happen? It'll be a laugh!'

'This was supposed to be a laugh,' I said, gesturing in the general direction of the party. 'It was supposed to be about us and our friends celebrating getting through the exams. Not about bloody Pete and his horrible friends.'

'If you had your way we'd all still be having a slumber party, watching a Barbie movie in our pyjamas,' Ellen snapped. 'Not all of us want to stay eight years old forever.'

In spite of myself I felt the tears welling up in my eyes. Trying to keep my voice steady, I repeated, 'I just wanted this to be about us and our friends. Why can't you stay, Ellen, and let them all leave if they want to?'

Ellen didn't answer. We stood in silence for a minute.

Pete appeared at the sitting room door. 'You ready, Ellen?'

'Yeah.' She moved towards him, then turned back and made one final plea. 'Please Maggie, come with us.'

The lump in my throat was so big I didn't trust myself to speak. I had lied for her, skipped school for her, almost got arrested for her. I'd had enough. I shook my head, watching an expression of resignation cross her face. She shrugged. 'Well, bye then.' And taking Pete's hand, she walked out, closing the door quietly behind her.

She had let me down so many times I don't know why it still surprised me. I suppose I still wanted to believe she was the same person underneath but the truth was the friend I had grown up with was already gone for good even before she walked out that door.

I didn't want to risk going up to Carrie's parents' room again. There was a queue for the main bathroom, and the one downstairs stank of vomit. I went and sat on the stairs.

That's where Liam found me. He came and sat beside me and took my hand in his without saying a word. I wanted to enjoy it, to remember exactly how it felt, his long slender fingers, his strong warm palm pressed against mine, but my heart was already too full.

Dear Ellen,

Today I kept thinking about that snow globe Mum always takes out at Christmas. It's an old-fashioned village scene, with a Christmas tree in the middle, decorated with red baubles. Just like that snow globe, someone has picked the real world up, and shaken it, so hard that the snow looks more like a fog, spreading out, covering everything. And then it starts to settle, but everything has moved, shifted position very slightly, and nothing is in its proper place any more.

Love,

Maggie.

I went home soon after Ellen left. I called a taxi and went to sit on the wall outside while I waited for it.

At home I tapped on my parents' door to let them know I was home, hearing my mother's murmur in reply. Then I got straight into bed, not even brushing my teeth or taking off my make-up for probably the first time ever. I didn't even get undressed, just took off my shoes and crawled under the duvet.

I heard the phone ringing some time after that. It was so late the first rays of morning sunshine were already touching the sky. The phone rang and rang. Only half awake, I pulled the pillow over my head and willed my parents to pick it up, and get rid of whatever idiot was calling.

I heard my mother's voice, sounding irritated and confused. And then suddenly clearer, sharper, jerking me properly awake. A clatter as she dropped the phone and then footsteps running towards my room. I sat up in bed, hugging the blankets to me so my mother wouldn't see that I was still wearing my clothes from last night. I don't know why I thought that still mattered.

'Maggie!' It was the first time in years that my mum had come into my room without knocking. 'That's Ellen's mum on the phone. Where is Ellen?'

And even as I tried to help, spoke to Ellen's mum on the phone and told her all I knew, even then there was a part of me that knew I would never know the answer to that question again.

Dear Ellen,

Why, why, why did you have to leave the party that night? I just can't get my head around how different things might have been if you'd just stayed. All those what ifs and if onlys and why didn't I stop you – they're swirling round my brain again, torturing me.

What's the worst thing that could happen? Oh Ellen, you had no idea.

Maggie.

I don't know exactly what happened after Ellen left the party. I wasn't there. But I've seen it in my mind so many times I feel like I was. It's like a film reel in front of my eyes, playing on a loop, over and over, and the only way to deal with it was just to turn it off.

Ellen sitting in the front seat of that clapped-out old banger of Pete's. Sitting on Spider's knee because Pete insisted on cramming eight of them into the car. All of them swigging from bottles of beer and singing along to the radio and yelling at Pete to go faster, faster. And that bend in the road that Pete didn't see coming, that other car travelling in the other direction. Pete taking the bend too quickly and meeting the other car head on. The awful, awful smash, the shattering of glass, the screeching of brakes far too late, the squealing of metal folding in on itself. And my best friend Ellen flying, flying straight out the windscreen, for just a moment seeming to float, suspended in the air, before smashing back to earth.

Dear Ellen,

David talked a lot again yesterday, about this not being a

linear process, about ups and downs and rollercoasters and setbacks, and slowly slowly making progress.

I went back to school today. People had obviously been told to be nice to me. Again. Siobhan Brady lent me her log tables when I couldn't find mine, and Carrie asked me to have lunch with her and Stephanie. We went to this new place on the main street. They do bagels and smoothies and that sort of thing. I had a cinnamon bagel with cream cheese and a raspberry smoothie. Carrie told us this story about Jane ringing up this boy she likes and his mother answering his mobile and interrogating her for half an hour. Stephanie was in stitches and suddenly I found myself laughing too. Afterwards I felt guilty, but I know I can't go through the rest of my life thinking I'll never have fun with anyone but you.

After school Liam came over to help me with some homework, and he asked me if I'd like to go ice skating at the weekend. I said I would. Mum's face lit up when I told her.

Bye for now,

Maggie.

What haunted me for a long time was that Ellen had no ID on her that night, so the guards weren't able to identify her right away. And of course her mother wasn't waiting for her to come home because she thought she was with me. Ellen lay in that cold hospital morgue for hours until that nice guard, Declan, came on his shift and heard what had happened. He of course recognised her right away when he saw her photo. He must have blamed himself too, maybe even more than Liam and I did. He was the one who drove out to Ellen's mother's house and asked her if she would come down to the hospital with him, gently explaining why. What an awful thing for him to have to do. Mrs B went into shock, insisting Ellen was safe and sound in my house, and rang my mum, expecting to be able to put Ellen on the phone right away so she could tell Declan herself that she was fine. I just can't bear to think about how she must have felt when my mum said that Ellen wasn't there and she had to face up to what Declan was telling her.

Dear Ellen,

I haven't written here for a while. I gave this notebook to David to read, and we talked about it afterwards. He didn't seem as surprised by any of it as I thought he might be, but I guess that's his job anyway. I've been seeing him a lot recently. It's helping. I used to think nothing ever would.

The other person I've been seeing a lot of is Liam. You probably guessed that anyway, but I wanted to tell you. He is everything I thought he would be Ellen, kind and funny and always so considerate, and best of all he's my friend too. We have even talked a little bit about you and how we miss you but we both believe we'll see you again one day. Actually just as he said that (we were walking through the park) the sun came out from behind a cloud, and it was almost like a sign from you, Ellen. Wherever you are I think you're at peace now and I feel like you're not angry at me for living my life.

I've started looking at college courses. It's not for a while of course, but I want to have an idea of where I'll go, and what I should be doing for my portfolio. There are so many art and design courses to choose from in England, but I think I'll probably go to Dublin, it'll be nice to be able to come home at weekends.

I still miss you, Ellen, and the things we used to do together, and the things we were going to do together. But I know I need to let you go.

Always your friend,

Maggie.